WHA

BECOME

Jacqueline Druga

PRESS

VULPINE
P R E S S

Published by Vulpine Press in the United Kingdom in 2020

Cover by Christian Bentulan

ISBN: 978-1-83919-044-5

www.vulpine-press.com

Also by Jacqueline Druga:

No Man's Land

When Leah and Calvin found out they were expecting, they were over the moon. That day would be one to remember forever... but for more reasons than one. That was the day the world changed. That was the day joy turned to fear. A deadly virus broke out, with many of those infected becoming violent and uncontrollable. And it was spreading fast.

The Last Woman

After emerging from a coma, Faye Wills opens her eyes to complete darkness and the feeling of being trapped. She awakens in the worst place imaginable, one of thousands of bodies in a makeshift mass grave that was once a football stadium.

Left for dead, there are no signs of life and the only sound she hears is the buzzing of flies that follow the stench of death.

Once out of the stadium she steps into a desolate, barren world, void of all life and people. Faye learns that while in a comatose state, the world was besieged by some sort of epidemic. Without a soul around, there are a lot of missing pieces. Where did everyone go?
In her weakened state, she must pull it together and move forward to find answers and survivors. However, she soon realizes that she may never find anyone and must face the possibility that she may be The Last Woman on earth.

ONE

NEW

Over the warm, small serving of potatoes, I acquired my first true glimpse of what we had become. The bowl was buried in my hands and for the first few spoonfuls I never raised my eyes. Shoveling it into my mouth like some sort of convict in a prison, protecting my food.

I clenched the spoon in my hand the same way I'd clench the handlebar of a bike. When I was younger my father would have a fit if he saw me holding my spoon like that.

"We aren't savages," he would say.

No. We weren't. Little did any of us know, we were savages in the making.

What choice did we have?

In some way and some part of us, no matter how hard we tried, we all had savage instincts.

The way I consumed my meager meal at that moment was savage.

It didn't matter what it looked like, or tasted like, I was hungry.

It was the first time since it had all started that I felt true hunger. I imagined it was nothing compared to what others had felt.

The potatoes were smashed, I guess to make them go further. They were seasoned with something, because they weren't bland.

Everyone seemed to have potatoes. Everyone I'd come across had them as if they were some sort of golden ticket.

In a sense they were. They were a means of survival.

The clack of my spoon against the ceramic dish made me pause, and I just stared down.

My fingers poked through holes in the knit gloves. They were so cold my fingertips looked white. I pulled my sweater from the sleeves of my coat to cover my hands, and that was when I peered up.

They all stared at me, and for a brief moment I felt guilty for eating. Was I taking from them? I was the stranger and the entertainment. Something to look at, I suppose.

It was mostly women and kids, a few men. We sat in a small room lit by candles. The building was big, but it was night, no sun. We all huddled together, and candlelight was a means to stay warm and alive.

My mouth hovering over my next bite, I glanced at their faces. Aside from different genders and ages, they all were so much alike. Splotches of black dirt smeared across their foreheads, noses and cheeks. Soot from the candle smoke and fires, from not bathing, from not caring. Blankets covered their shoulders and their eyes glistened in the dancing light of the candle.

It was quiet, except for a few sniffles and the howling wind that seeped through the cracks in the walls and windows making an eerie whistling sound.

I was grateful for them.

For the meal and shelter shared out of kindness.

Out of humanity.

It wasn't lost. Not yet. It would be eventually.

To see those in the room, one would think they had lived scared, hungry and freezing for months or even years.

Sadly, it had only been weeks and we were still in the beginning of it all.

If this was what we had become, I shuddered to think where we'd end up.

TWO

MINIMUM

July 4
Six Weeks Earlier

I was sure the people at Maestro Ice thought my husband, Glen, was nuts. Even I thought he had lost it when he told me that he and his two buddies had ordered a thousand pounds of sculpting ice. Those giant ice blocks weighed two hundred pounds each and set them back a lot of money.

Glen said, "It'll be worth it. Trust me."

I replied with my stock, *Hmm.*

We had been together so long that nothing much really shocked me and, in a way, I welcomed it when something did.

He was predictable. I was predictable.

The blocks of ice were a nice change of pace; I was convinced the three of them were going to attempt to sculpt. After all, they were the best carpenters I knew, and if they could shape wood, surely they could shape ice.

But art wasn't why he'd ordered it. A keen foresight was the reason. Following what was considered the harshest, coldest winter in over a hundred years, we faced a summer that rivaled the drought of 1988. Long streaks of hot weather with no rain and high humidity.

It was so bad the whole house AC didn't even make that big of a dent. Unless, of course, you were outside, got good and hot and went indoors, then you felt it…briefly. Glen had gone to his aunt's house and retrieved an old air conditioner from thirty years ago, cranked it with whatever they put in it to make the air cooler and put it in our bedroom. We slept well and cold.

We never lost our roots or forgot where we came from. Other than the house we'd bought, we lived within our means. I remembered all too well when we were young, married and Aaron was a toddler. A pound of ground beef was two meals for us when mixed with Ramen noodles and tomatoes. It wasn't bad.

We traded our two-bedroom apartment for a better one when Glen started working for Markland Construction. His side jobs turned into his own business and we celebrated Aaron's tenth birthday in our very first home. One we owned proudly and made into our dream house. We added a pool and a garage with an in-law apartment for his mom—which wasn't exactly my dream situation—and a sister for Aaron. Although, at twelve, he was a little old to appreciate Cleo when she was born. We finally stopped working on the house feeling somewhat satisfied with it when Cleo was three.

I wanted badly to get rid of the pool and fill it in. It scared me having a pool with a baby. Glen fenced it in with an alarm that rang every time the gate was opened.

Annoying, but it gave me peace of mind.

That pool would have been a saving grace in the heat had it not been too warm to enjoy during the day. At night it helped.

The heat was unbearable.

I didn't understand why Glen wanted to have our Fourth of July picnic outdoors. I argued to have it inside.

He had a plan.

After firing up the grill to heat—a grill we didn't need, I swore we could cook on the patio slate—he and his two buddies Bruce and Jim took off.

I had no idea where they went.

Bruce's and Jim's wives sat with me at the patio table under the umbrella that wasn't making a dent in the heat. The kids were inside, I could see them through the glass doors. I wanted to take my margarita inside as well, but I had to watch the grill.

Glen said they'd be right back.

I swear I was the only one the heat got to. The pool looked so inviting, but I knew if I went in, it would be like taking a bath.

Anna and Jill chatted away. I nodded, occasionally smiled but couldn't stop thinking about how hot it was. I had one of those fans that blew water on me. I kept lifting it, spraying myself and grunting in heated frustration.

"Mackenzie," Jill said my name with a chuckle. "Don't think about the heat and it won't bother you."

"Don't think about it?" I asked. "Are you serious? It's a hundred and five. I can't have my phone out here."

"Well, it won't be for long," said Anna.

"We're on day thirty-one," I said.

"You're counting?" Anna asked, laughing. "Three more days. They have that cold front in Canada, we're supposed to get it in a couple days."

"Cold front." I shook my head. "Yeah, it'll drop to ninety."

"Still cooler than it is now," Anna replied.

I brought my margarita to my lips; the frozen beverage wasn't surviving. I'd down it and make another. I had to check on Cleo anyhow. She was only five and Aaron's teenage attention span to watch her wasn't a guarantee. "I'm gonna check on Cleo," I said and started to stand when I saw my mother-in-law making her way across the lawn from her apartment. She held a large bowl in her hands, and I couldn't figure out why she was wearing a sweater.

"Girls," Helen said. "Having fun?"

"Joining us, Mrs. Garret?" Anna asked.

"Oh, no not me, I'm watching my shows," Helen replied.

"Why are you wearing a sweater, Helen?" I asked. "You're gonna get heat stroke."

"Not me." She reached out and grabbed my arm. "Feel, Mac." Her hands were like ice.

"What the heck?" I jumped a little. "You're like dead cold."

"You wish."

"Hmm," I hummed out and took a sip.

"Glen needs to fix my AC. It's too cold in my place," she said. "I told him, but he's always busy with something you need him to do. I'm going to take this to the kitchen. I made macaroni salad. I think I'll grab one of those drinks if you don't mind."

"No, not at all," I told her. "Can you check on Cleo? Make sure she's okay. Aaron is watching her."

"Aaron is great with her. Why do you worry?" She leaned down and touched my forehead. "You need to get out of the sun. You're burning up. You're the one who will get heat stroke."

"Tell me about it. Maybe I'll go to your place and cool down."

"You'll regret it. I'm sitting under a blanket."

As my mother-in-law slipped into the house, I looked at my friends. There was no way her place was that cold. I was about to go

7

and find out, but when I stood, I saw Glen's truck. He pulled into the driveway then backed up to the fence, dripping water the whole time.

It was at that second I understood why he'd purchased that ice.

They were comical moving the slippery blocks from the back end of the truck. They even dropped one. But after twenty minutes with everyone outside cheering them on…they did it.

It was a stroke of brilliancy: he was putting it in the pool. I wasn't really sure how much a thousand pounds of ice would cool down our small, underground pool but it was a great effort.

The ice melted pretty quickly in the water, just like my margarita. But just like my margarita, I was going to absorb what relief from the heat I could.

I was the first one in the pool, jumping in without hesitation. Maybe it was psychological, but it felt cold and so good against my burning skin. Doing something I rarely do, I joked about the floating chunks of ice and feeling like I was in the *Titanic* movie.

No one really laughed. It wasn't that funny, but at that moment, for the first time in thirty-one days, I was cold. I enjoyed it because I knew, with the summer the way it was going, it was going to be a long time before I was cold again.

THREE

CHANGE

July 7

Being a deep sleeper, it took a lot to wake me up, especially if it had only been a couple hours. The night before I'd sat in the basement family room, which was much cooler, and binge-watched on a streaming station until a little after three.

Then I went to bed fully intent on sleeping in and not setting the alarm.

Yet, there I was feeling like the comforter had been ripped from me. But it hadn't been. I was always a cover-heavy person. I liked to be cold when I slept, snug under some heavy covers. It wasn't the case in the summer. The bed sported our hot weather bedding that was light and airy. Not as heavy and snug as I preferred. The bedspread with only a top sheet worked well with the air conditioner. But not on this morning.

I was so cold and shivering I thought the covers weren't on me. When I realized they were, I groaned out, "Oh my God, turn down the air."

For sure it had to be his super-charged AC from decades ago. That thing was a monster.

I didn't get a response and I opened my eyes. It was barely eight in the morning and the loud buzz and hum of the old AC wasn't ringing out.

The room was quiet.

I sat up.

Glen wasn't in bed. His side had the covers tossed back. I thought it was earlier than it was because it wasn't bright out. The days had been bright and sunny, but on this day, it was gloomy.

Need I say it was welcome? After weeks with sun and heat, I was so happy to see it was overcast. That meant lower temperatures and possibly rain. I swore I was going to go stand in the yard the first instance of rain.

It was probably too late. I could hear it hitting against the window.

What a difference the beating sun must have made to the temperature of the house.

I couldn't believe how cold it felt. Perhaps it was my imagination.

Since I was already up, I put on my slippers, grabbed a pair of sweatpants from my drawer and a sweater from my closet. I was sure Glen would poke fun at me, telling me I reminded him of his mother.

A nap was on the agenda for the afternoon before I'd even walked from my bedroom.

I could smell the coffee the second I stepped into the hall and I followed the aroma down to the kitchen.

"Morning," I heard Glen say from the dining room. "You're up early."

"Imagine that. You aren't working today?" I asked as I grabbed a mug.

"Not today."

"Okay." I poured some coffee, added my creamer and, cupping the mug with both hands, headed into the dining room. I expected to see him at the table, peering at his phone, going through emails or reading the news. Instead my husband stood at the sliding glass doors, staring out while bringing his mug to his lips and drinking his coffee.

Wondering if he saw something interesting out there or maybe his mother had another 'friend' over, I joined him.

"What are you doing?" I asked.

"Wondering if I should put the furnace on."

I laughed. He had made a joke.

Or had he?

Glen was drop-dead serious as he stared out.

"Glen, I know it's cooler but..." My eyes shifted when I heard the sound of the rain against the glass. It had a thin sound to it, like a fine mist rather than rain drops.

"It's cold," he said. "Look at the pool."

I did. A fog hovered over our in-ground pool. "Is that steam?"

"Yep. Temperature fell so fast this morning, the water temperature hadn't changed," he said.

"That's so strange. I mean it isn't that cold out." I brought my mug to my lips.

"Forty-six."

The sip I took nearly choked me. "You're kidding?"

"Nope. Why do you think I want to put the furnace on?"

"Surely it will go back up."

"It could."

"I say we deal with it, enjoy it, and hope the house stays cool as the temperature goes up."

"I looked online, Mac," Glen said. "When I woke up and saw the temp on my phone, I thought 'wow this is unusual' and it is. The coldest day in July on record was this temperature in Alaska. We're far from Alaska."

"Did you check Pennsylvania?"

"Yep and it's nowhere near this."

"It's early," I said. "The temperature will only rise today. It has to, it's July. Have you checked the news?"

"No. Not yet."

"Morning show is on until nine. They'll cover local weather." With my coffee in hand and my sleepy state leaving, I sat on the couch, grabbed the remote and turned on the television. I flipped to the network with the perky morning ladies. I expected to see them with a guest or cooking something, I didn't expect to see a major news anchor with a map of the United States superimposed behind him. "Glen. Come look at this."

There had to be a mistake. Dramatics. I wasn't listening—the volume was down. They cut to a reporter wearing a hat and coat. The wind was blowing and steam came from her mouth when she spoke.

Were they showing a pre-recorded spot?

Was the media looking to hype something that wasn't there? It was July. The hottest summer on record, yet I was looking at a weather map that made me think it was January.

I felt the bounce of the couch as Glen sat down.

"Thank you, Canada, for sharing," Glen said quietly.

"Was it this cold there?" I asked.

Glen shrugged. "According to that map, it's still cold there."

I looked at my husband, then back to the television just as it returned to the anchor.

Glen took the remote and raised the volume.

"You would think," the newscaster said, "that was Molly reporting in November, but that was live footage. No one is really certain why such a brutal cold front has descended on the northern portion of the US. But, folks, it is here for a while. Don't make any plans to go swimming, because if you think it's cold now, it's about to get colder. A lot colder. And it looks like…" The newscaster paused. "It's only the beginning."

<><><><>

The entire day we took things in our stride, even going as far as to make jokes. The cold, damp weather, combined with a warm ground created a dense fog. One tricky to drive or move around in. We needed to, though.

It was a good day for soup so we went to the store. I didn't know what people were thinking or if they had heard things. I thought maybe the market was having one of their 'super sales' the parking lot was so packed. People rushed to get inside and Glen had to search the lot for a cart. There was no sale which brought me back to my original thought if people had heard a newsflash that we hadn't. The store was insane, and the lines extended way back. We were greeted immediately with the sight of half-empty shelves. Odd things like ketchup and canned tomatoes were out. It was crazy. Shoppers were treating a freak cold day like it was the day before a snow day in the winter.

Panic shopping.

I kept checking online.

Were we missing something?

Nothing indicated it was more than just a few days of freakishly cold July weather.

Soup and grilled cheese sandwiches were the dinner I planned, a good winter meal in the middle of July.

I baked cookies to keep the house warm and the moisture from the soup helped. About the time the soup had simmered to perfection, I heard the triple click and whirl of the furnace.

Glen had conceded.

Never would I have believed we would put on the furnace in July. Yet there we were. I caught a whiff of that burning smell that always seemed to accompany the first time the furnace was on for the season.

Nothing about it felt right to me, yet the news was reporting it was just some anomaly.

The only one it didn't seem to faze was Helen. I kept expecting her to tell me she remembered a time when it was this cold. She was always one to give that 'been there, done that' story to quell any worries. But the stories of 'this happened before' never came.

By nightfall, the temperature hovered just above freezing and the fog was thick. So much so, Helen had to spend the night in the house with us; it was too dangerous to walk across the lawn. We couldn't even see her apartment.

It seemed silly—I felt silly—breaking out the winter blankets and comforters. However, it was just too cold. Perhaps it was the weeks of exceptionally hot weather that had made us more intolerable. There was no adjustment period like when we would go from fall to winter.

Sweating one day with an air-conditioning system that didn't seem to do the trick, to shivering with icy cold hands the next.

This extreme.

It was fast.

And I was grateful it was a freak of nature and wouldn't last long.

FOUR

QUEUE

July 14

It was strange. All everyone talked about was the bizarre cold front that took over everything north of Kentucky the first week of July. A cold front they predicted would spread south.

It was on social media, the news. People kept panic shopping, going every day. The stores assured everyone there was no shortage of food. Yet there were those who were extreme. Though, they weren't the norm…at least for the first couple days. Then the snow came. It never stuck—it melted right away—but it was steady and didn't stop.

The blue skies were gone and every day was gray and dismal.

When would it end?

Then things really started to get crazy.

People literally believed it was the end of the world. Levelheaded people spewed irrational thoughts and fear consumed them.

At work, that was all everyone talked about. When people showed up, that was. People stopped going to work everywhere. I worked for a local magistrate and every day more cases were cancelled.

Things spiraled to a doomsday mentality and I didn't get it.

Even though experts said it was just a spell, some worried it was much more. That we were being lied to and placated.

My mother-in-law was one of them. In fact, she was horrible with her conspiracy theories and bickered with me. They weren't even scientific theories, they were her own mental guesses.

She constantly argued with us that we needed to go south.

"For what?" I asked

"It's only gonna get colder. Uncle Fred has a house in Georgia. Bet it's warm there."

"We don't need to go to Georgia. But if you want to," I said, "be my guest."

"Can't go to Aunt Mary's. She lives in Florida."

"I would think Florida is even better," I said.

"No, before long it will be under water."

"Where are you getting this from?" I asked.

She replied with a, "You'll see," but nothing to corroborate her theory until she actually made a point one day with a paper cup.

It was the day I believe she caught my attention.

A lot changed that day.

She made her way across the lawn, carrying this saran-covered, plastic Solo Cup. She wore her favorite beige raincoat and a plastic, red polka dot rain bonnet.

She had a couple of those bonnets, courtesy of my son, Aaron. They were his go-to Christmas and birthday gifts since she proclaimed to love them so much.

I kind of think she did. She wore them all the time.

Aaron always found her amusing and fed into her eccentricities and quirkiness.

"Mr. Richter," Helen said smugly.

"Who is Mr. Richter?" I asked.

"My fourth-grade science teacher."

"My God, what a memory," I said. "That was ages ago."

"Ma," Aaron said. "Gram is smart."

"Thank you, honey," Helen said. "You're the best."

"So are you, Gram."

"Christ," I mumbled and returned my attention to the small kitchen television.

"Oh, am I bothering you?" Helen asked. "You asked me a question two days ago and I am here to answer it. I just had to have proof."

"Okay." I faced her. "I'm all ears. What was the question?"

"You asked where I was getting my information when I said everything was going to flood."

"Okay." I nodded.

"Mr. Richter," she said.

"Your fourth-grade science teacher. Don't tell me he's still alive."

"Go on with that sas," she said. "I remember him telling me that it takes three inches of rain to equal one inch of snow. I remember a big snowstorm one year and he said we were lucky it was snow or we'd give Noah a run for his flood money."

"I highly doubt that," I said. "But go on."

She placed the cup on the counter and lifted the plastic wrap.

I peered in. "It's water."

"Yes, it is," she replied. "Actually, it's snow. Snow melts. It's been snowing steadily for an entire day. Twenty-four hours and the snow just falls and melts. This was placed outside this morning. There is five inches of water in here. It's an inch an hour."

"Holy shit," Aaron blurted.

"Aaron," I scolded on his language.

18

"No, that's smart, Gram."

Helen nodded. "There's no evaporation because it keeps coming. An inch an hour." She gave a twitch of her head. "Take a look at your pool."

With a slow side step, I moved by Helen and my son toward the patio doors.

I looked out and released a slight gasp. The water in my pool was nearly to the edge.

"Any higher," Helen said, "I may have to break out the galoshes."

I just kept staring.

"Two more days," Helen added. "It's gonna flood the drainage system. The rivers, creeks. If it keeps going like this, we'll need to go south. I'm not saying to higher ground, but maybe."

"That just seems so extreme." I was in a daze, staring at the water, the large, falling snowflakes that disappeared as soon as they hit the pool. I was starstruck by the weather, so much so that when Glen's truck whizzed into the driveway, splashing the water, I jumped.

Why was he driving so fast?

"Is that dad?" Aaron asked.

"Yeah," I replied. I watched Glen step out of the truck as he carried one canvas grocery store bag.

He walked around toward the front of the house, avoiding the backyard and I went back to the kitchen.

"He's been gone awhile," Aaron said.

"I know." I heard the front door open and then Cleo calling out excitedly for her father.

With our five-year-old on his hip, Glen entered the kitchen and placed the bag on the counter.

"You were gone a really long time," I said.

"Yeah. It sucks," Glen replied.

"Glen?" I looked in the bag. "Is this it? Did you forget the list?"

"No, that…" Glen set down Cleo and whispered to her, "Go watch TV, honey." He looked at me and reached into the bag. "This is all we're allowed."

"What?" I asked in shock. "What do you mean?"

"We're not permitted to shop. I guess to stop the hoarders. I don't know."

"There was nothing on the news."

Glen shrugged. "I don't know what to tell you. It's the way it is. I had to wait in line for a prepackaged bag of groceries. Three days, family of four."

"Five," Helen corrected.

"Sorry, Mom," Glen said. "You and Cleo count as half a person each."

"Wait. Stop." I waved out my hand. "They told you what you can get?"

"More like they just handed us what we could have."

"That makes no sense," I said. "Did they say why?"

"No one gave me any answers, Mac. It's just the way it is."

"I can't accept that," I argued. "I can't."

"I don't know what to tell you," Glen replied. "I don't."

"Maybe if you try another store. You probably misunderstood or went to the wrong place. Did you try Big Bear?"

"Mac," he said my name with a snap to it. "It's that way everywhere. Okay? I don't know what you want me to tell you. It is the way it is. Why do you think this is on me?"

"I just…I just would have tried elsewhere," I said. "One of the smaller markets. Maybe the big ones are just falling into line."

"Falling into line of what?" Glen asked. "This isn't a conspiracy theory, this is a national emergency. They have to control things."

20

"So we're just supposed to accept it?" I asked.

"What choice do we have?" Glen responded. "The stores are basically shut down."

"They give you a bag of nothing, but you can't touch the shelves?"

"No," Glen said. "From what I saw the shelves were bare. It was weird. And it wasn't even the workers, it was like government people," Glen said.

"They can't do that," I argued.

"They can," Helen stated. "They will and they did."

"Oh, please." My eyes rolled slightly as I looked at her, facially showing how ridiculous I thought her response was. Over the top, just like Helen.

"Where is all the food?" Aaron asked. "I mean, there are warehouses, why didn't they restock the shelves?"

"I'll tell you why," Helen interjected. "The government seized all the food. Probably doing some sort of major foraging and moving the items south. Have to have items down there for all the people."

I huffed a little in disbelief, shaking my head.

"She's right," Glen said. "The government has taken control of food and warehouses to ship south. Mac..." he said my name softly. "There's a major evacuation in effect. I mean...turn on the news."

"Is it flooding?" Aaron asked.

"I don't know," Glen replied. "It definitely is weather related."

"Our city?" I questioned. "We have all those rivers and—"

"The entire north," Glen cut me off.

"North what?"

"America," Glen said. "Everyone must move below the southernmost part of the Mason–Dixon Line. It's like you take a line and draw it straight through Arkansas across the country."

His words made me nearly stumble in shock. "How are they going to evacuate the entire northern half. More than half?"

Glen shook his head. "Don't know. They said there is a schedule. In order to prevent a mass exodus. Every area will be given an evacuation time and location. You're supposed to put in your address and it tells you where to go and your evacuation date."

"State for state," Helen said. "City for city. Move us to a comparable area. Probably set up camps."

"We don't know," I said. "They're not even saying why."

"Isn't it obvious, Mom?" Aaron asked. "It's July. It's thirty-four degrees."

My son didn't need to say it. No one did. I knew the answer to that one. Only one thing coming would cause all of us to head south. Unimaginable, not survivable...cold."

It was all over the news that a government website would launch at eight that evening. I knew it was going to be a disaster, everyone going online at the same time. Half the country needed to know where they had to go and when.

Of course, unsurprisingly, we were unable to log on.

System overload.

Yet, according to social media, people were in and finding out the plan. Obviously, the site worked some place.

While I waited, I researched.

It was hard to believe something that big causing an evacuation was actually happening.

Every news site, every webpage, was all doom and gloom.

I couldn't even go down my social media feed without seeing something about it.

It was being called the 'Big Cold.' Similar to the last mini ice age, scientists were attributing it to something called a grand solar minimum. I wasn't exactly sure what that was, but it had to do with the sun's activity. It caused the last one.

We were expected to face the same, only colder.

The government was stating it was a precaution. Some said it was never going to happen, while some experts said it would be worse than we could imagine.

Those opinions, I dismissed. I didn't want to hear them.

I wanted to know if we had to leave. How long was it going to last? I found social media groups that were claiming they were riding it out and stating where.

The search for answers felt like one of those times I was hungry and couldn't find anything to satisfy that hunger even with a full fridge. Lots of information was out there, but nothing I wanted to hear and nothing that really told me much.

Admittedly, I sought out options that called the Big Cold ludicrous. That it was all hype. Some sort of political thing. The government's way of controlling people.

But why would they move everybody if it was? We weren't the only country doing it, either. This thing was global.

It was quickly put together…too fast. As if they'd known it was coming for some time.

They were moving entire neighborhoods to a single location. I read online a prison in Texas was holding one thousand, four hundred and twelve residents from an Ohio town.

Prisons, makeshift camps, arenas, schools, everything was being used.

My next-door neighbor got online. She told me once you put in your address, your evacuation location appeared along with your leave date. Then, after that you filled in details and registered.

She left a few things out.

Maybe she didn't want to give me too much information in case I was never able to get in.

I worried for a bit. What if we never found out our location? Then just before four in the morning, I was able to log in. I waited in a queue for nearly an hour after I put in our address.

I was nervous.

Then it popped up.

RCGA-223. Relocation Camp 223, Bainbridge, Georgia.

The note said, 'under construction.' I didn't know what that entailed, but I was glad it wasn't a prison.

After I registered the family and names, the rules were displayed. A copy, they politely stated, would be emailed to me. Just like an airplane, no more than one bag and one personal item per person, and it gave the measurements.

Food was permitted to be brought into camp in a duffle bag no longer than thirty-six inches. We also were allowed to bring one aluminum briefcase with personal documents and items. The case had to be purchased.

If anything over the allotment was brought to camp, we would be asked to leave it behind.

How in the world does one fit their entire life into a backpack and small suitcase?

We had to up and leave our home and life to go to some strange place. With no say whatsoever where we went.

The strict rules and relocation policies were to avoid chaos and mass hysteria.

I wanted to cry.

Then I saw our evacuation date.

September 14. That was two months away.

I breathed out in relief.

Whatever was happening, this...Big Cold wasn't as severe as they were saying, it couldn't be. Not if they were giving us a two-month heads-up.

And a lot could happen in two months.

I was siding with the naysayers and putting my faith in the hope that the Big Cold was going to be one of those media hypes like Y2K or 2012 and come September we wouldn't be leaving...we'd be laughing about it.

FIVE

RED RUBBER BOOTS

August 1

Packing up our things wasn't even a thought or option, nor would it have been for a while had the weather not taken such a drastic turn. Odd storms would move in at night, bringing severe winds, lightning and falling temperatures. It was impossible to leave at night, everything froze over and when it started to defrost during the day, the falling snow just turned everything on the ground into slush. Until it froze over again. A daily occurrence of rinse and repeat weather.

Helen was the only one thinking ahead. Scraping a thing or two from our three-day rations, going through what she had in her own cupboards to see what she could compact into her personal bag.

Truth was, the amount of food given wasn't enough and any extra we had in our pantries was dwindling, especially when they switched the ration days to once a week and did so without notice.

Everything changed fast. We went from being free to being regimented. Only essential services worked, which left my job as a magistrate clerk obsolete. Suddenly, my view of the world changed. I went from being out there daily to stuck in my house, fighting every urge I had not to become one of those millions who were freaking out.

The circumstances they threw at us didn't help. Rolling blackouts occurred during the day to conserve power. We were given a day and time to collect our rations—if we missed it, we didn't get anything for a week.

Fuel purchase was regulated to the bare minimum in an attempt to keep people from joining the already-congested roads for the exodus.

When it was your time to go, you would be given enough fuel.

No one worked and no one had money.

A way to control everything.

It wasn't that way everywhere. Just in places that were to be evacuated.

While we were in a police state, everywhere else lived normally.

They weren't happy about the exodus or sharing their areas.

There were social media groups complaining, petitions being signed. I feared for my family when we did go. Helen kept insisting we go to her brother's. As crazy as he was, it was better. Plus, he was in Georgia so we would be on our designated route.

My kids were tougher than I was. Cleo took everything in her stride and spent the days doing things a five-year-old would do. Not paying attention or caring about what was going on.

Aaron didn't want to know. He hid that he was a little sad when they cancelled school. I guessed at seventeen that had more to do with not seeing his friends.

I was constantly online looking for answers. I wasn't even sure of the questions in my mind, I just needed information. It couldn't be happening, it didn't make any sense.

Glen worked, though. He took a job doing contract work for the government building check-in stations on the highway. It didn't pay cash—it paid commodities such as fuel—and once the project was done he earned extra food bags. He wouldn't have taken it just for cash. Money had lost its value.

I hadn't been out of the house in weeks. Not since they told me not to go to work and never called me back.

That had to change.

It was pushing three o'clock, Glen wasn't home. He phoned to say he wouldn't be home for a while and if we didn't get to the store for our ration pick up we were shit out of luck for a week.

We didn't have enough food to go another week.

I had to leave the house.

Aaron offered to go with me so I took him up on it.

"Take a pair of my boots," Helen told me. "I have enough."

"I really don't need the boots," I replied. "I'm going from the car to the store and back."

"Take my boots. They have steel toes."

"What the hell do red rubber boots have steel toes for?" I asked.

"Weight. That helps. Weight makes traction. Take my boots."

We went back and forth and finally I relented. Helen gave me this hideous pair of red rubber boots. They came halfway up my calves and I looked ridiculous.

Helen stayed with Cleo, and Aaron and I loaded into my little wagon, one of those small SUVs with barely a back hatch.

I didn't know what to expect. Once outside, I felt strange. Bundled in my winter coat, I forgot it was summer. It was so cold.

Living north, driving in bad weather wasn't usually an issue, but I wasn't mentally prepared for my car to slide the second I pulled from the driveway. Not with all-wheel drive.

I thought watery slush was hard to get traction, but I could feel the ice crunching beneath my tires and I drove at a snail's pace.

"You okay, Mom?" Aaron asked.

"Yeah, just, you know, nervous."

"Want me to drive?" he asked.

I only glanced briefly at him as my response.

"Did you ever think it would be like this?"

"No," I answered, focusing on the road.

"Everything's changed, Mom. I mean, nothing will ever be the same."

"I'm still not convinced that it is going to stay," I said. "I researched the last mini ice age. It happened in the 1800s. Started with a volcano, but they never went south."

"That we know of. That was centuries ago."

When he said that, it made me cringe. Centuries. So much had changed technology wise, it was hard to know what they did or didn't do.

"I think this is it," Aaron said. "The moment the world changes. It'll never be the same. I won't grow up in a stable world."

"Aaron, don't say that."

"It's true. I mean in a month we're packing our things and leaving our home to run from the cold."

"See that's what doesn't make sense," I said. "A month. We don't leave for a month, so much could change. How can they know things won't get better?"

"Or they could get worse."

When he said that, my windshield wipers cleared the snow and my tires created a wave as I drove through a slush puddle, sending up a huge amount of water to the side of the road.

That should have been reiteration enough for me.

Just as I turned onto Conner I had to stop. Police blocked the parking lot entrance and there was a mob of people on the road, yelling and screaming, trying to get to the store.

"Mom?" Aaron questioned.

"How the hell are we supposed to get into Stockey's?"

I found myself unable to drive through. I beeped. No one would move, so I backed up and pulled over.

"We're gonna walk through that?" Aaron asked

"Straight through to the store. The reason people are doing this is because they can't get in," I said. "It's our day. We can."

"So we think."

We both got out of the car. I locked the doors, secured my purse with the strap over my head and diagonally across my chest. I focused on the store, staying close to Aaron, at times grabbing on to his arms. It was at that moment I realized how much water was on the street as my feet splashed in the slush. The boots were heavy and Helen was right, it helped. Except the steel in the toe got awfully cold.

All those people were standing in it.

It's cold, go home, I thought, *stay warm, wait your turn.* I got it, I did. They barely gave enough food. There was nothing that could be done and screaming in the streets wasn't going to change a thing.

Then Aaron started yelling, tossing his fist in the air. "Unfair! We deserve food."

I nudged him with my hand. "What the hell are you doing?"

"I don't want to stand out. Not be the only ones not protesting."

I wasn't sure how much of a good idea that was but, luckily, it didn't take us long to get to the lot.

We were told several times by officers to step back, despite us saying it was our day. I started to think that maybe that was the reason for the protests, that they weren't letting anyone in. Then finally, someone listened, checked my identification and let us through into the lot.

That was step one.

We still had to stand outside in line to get into the store. While it wasn't bitter cold, standing out there took its toll. My ungloved hands were frozen over and my ears hurt. Our pick-up time was three o'clock, but it pushed four by the time we stepped foot inside the store.

Five at a time.

Were they serious?

I thought they'd hand us a bag and send us on our way. Instead, they handed us several empty bags to fill. Stations were set up. We were to pick three meats, three starches, canned fruit, a cereal and measly gallon of milk to last a week. Although the powdered stuff was there for our taking. The only item that was plentiful was potatoes. We were given a large, heavy sack.

One small bin had tomatoes, most looked horrible but I spotted a good one. Reaching for it, I paused when a woman nearly snatched it from my hand. It was insane. It was a tomato. But how long would it be until we saw another fresh tomato?

"This reminds me of the food bank," Aaron said, grabbing a box of macaroni and cheese.

"When were you at the food bank?" I asked.

"With the Davidsons. I went with Greg to pick up their order."

"The Davidsons needed a food bank. I didn't know."

"Mom, a lot of people need the food bank," Aaron said. "And food stamps. I'm willing to bet these bags of food are more than some people usually have. At least everybody gets something, right? I know it seems like a shitty thing for the government to do, but if they didn't, how high would this store hike their prices? How many people wouldn't be able to get anything?"

When did my son become such a humanitarian? He didn't get it from me. The Davidsons were our next-door neighbors and I had no idea that they didn't have enough to eat.

Did any of us really pay attention to the needs of others?

"Jesus," I said. "How old are you? I think seventeen going on forty."

"Nah, that's just the future politician in me talking. I'm gonna make a difference or well, I was."

"Every politician starts out with good intentions."

"Doesn't matter now."

"It will. Trust me, it won't be this way for long."

My naivety spoke. Other than naive, I was pretty cynical.

I was happy my husband and children weren't.

We finished our 'pickings' and filled the three bags, picked up our sack of potatoes and the pre-filled bag, then left the store.

Getting to the store was easier than making our way back. The walk seemed longer and I felt vulnerable as we carried our items through the angry crowd. The snow was steady, the cold flakes beat against my face. Aaron carried the bags and I lugged the lone sack of potatoes.

We made it through, every few feet bumping into someone who was determined to storm their way to the store to make a statement, never seeing us as we made it against the grain.

Finally, the car was in sight. I hoped it would warm up fast. Juggling the potatoes to my other arm, I reached in my purse for my keys, and undid the locks

"We'll put them in the back," I said, then with another click of the key fob, the back hatch slowly raised and was open by the time we got there.

With a grunt I put my potatoes inside. "This will help with traction, I hope."

"Let's hope." Aaron put the last bag in. "You got it?" he asked about the hatch.

"Yep." I pressed the interior button that closed the hatch as my son walked to his side of the car.

It was normal. It was routine, something I did without thinking. Close the hatch, grab my keys, aim for the driver's door, when I noticed Aaron stopped and stared behind us.

"Mom, get in the car," he said. "Now."

Right then, I made two crucial mistakes.

I said, "What?"

"Mom. Now."

Then the second error was looking to see what he saw.

"Mom!"

Just as I noticed the two men and one woman, the men were already charging our way. I rushed as fast as I could to the driver's door, but the boots were heavy and I couldn't move as fast as I wanted to. Not that it would have mattered. When I reached the door, they reached me.

The one man blasted into me, hitting me hard with his shoulder, knocking me out of the way and to the ground.

"Mom!" Aaron screamed.

I was on the ground, on my side, stunned.

"Grab the keys," one of the men said.

"No. No," I sputtered, keeping those keys tight in my hand as I rolled to get up. As I did, I felt the foot slam into my face knocking me back down.

I could hear my son calling out, shouting something.

Everything happened fast and was a blur.

Adrenaline and fear were pumping rapidly through me, too much for me to feel the pain or cold as I splashed back to the freezing water.

It was the woman who kicked me. I saw her standing there. Hurriedly, I drew my hand toward me and she stomped on my arm, causing my fingers to uncurl.

"Got 'em," she said, snatching them out of my palm. "Let's go!"

One more, "No," came from me as I struggled to grab her, hold her leg, as if I could hold her back. I was weak, until I saw my son, trying his hardest to fight the man.

The man kept striking my son.

Over and over, brutally.

That was all I needed. I let go of the woman's pant leg.

Hurriedly, I pulled myself up, focusing on my son and trying to get to him.

It was gut wrenching to see my son take that beating.

Crying out, "No! leave him alone!" I charged my child's way, watching the man strike him again.

I knew I wasn't big enough to fight him. I just had to stop him. His cohorts yelled for him to hurry, and, slightly hunched, still grasping my son, he turned. When he did, I did the only thing I could think of. I revved back my leg and kicked him as hard as I could in the side of the knee.

I didn't expect the result I received.

The way he stood, the force of my emotionally driven kick combined with the steel toe hitting him directly in the right spot, I heard a crack a split second before he grunted and went down.

I didn't feel victorious, I felt angry, so enraged. I screamed, "You son of a bitch!" and kicked him again in the knee, then again in the leg. I started kicking him with my steel toe boots and just couldn't stop.

"Mom."

I was blinded by rage, everything was black and blurry and I kept kicking. Arms, chest…

"Mom. Stop."

Partially crying, I screamed with every blow I delivered…stomach…head…

"Mom!"

Face…head…head …

"Mom, stop!" Aaron grabbed me and pulled me back.

Breathing heavily, my shoulders bounced up and down. I couldn't think clearly. Looking at my son, seeing his badly beaten face made me want to scream even more.

"No!" I pulled away from his hold.

Then Aaron said my name with a whimper.

I looked to my right, my car was gone. Suddenly, I grew angry again, and turned my attention to the man. "You son of a…"

I stopped and felt every ounce of anger drain from my body when I looked down at him. He was on the ground, rolled somewhat on this side, half his face was submerged in the slush that was red with blood.

I stared into his eyes. His wide-open eyes.

"Mom," Aaron said. "We need to get him help."

I knew looking at him, there was no help to get him.

What did I do?

Me, a file clerk, homemaker and mother…had just brutally killed a man.

SIX

DAZED

Standing there absolutely numb, I didn't know how to react at first. Which scared me. I didn't like horror films or documentaries about killers. I was, for the most part, pretty squeamish. Yet, there I was standing over a dead body, a death caused by my hands, or rather...feet.

The first reaction I felt was shock, not that you feel shock, but I had to be in shock because all I worried about was my son's face. I saw the man but it hadn't really registered what I had done.

I worried about Aaron. Not even my own face, which I knew had to be injured.

His lip was already huge, the red on the side of his face started to bruise immediately. His left eye was beet red and his nose surely was broken.

My poor son.

Far too young to receive a beating like that from a grown man. Shock.

"Let me see, baby, let me see your face," I said.

"Mom, it's okay."

"No, it's not." Then I realized he probably wasn't feeling anything. Between the cold and the adrenaline, physically, Aaron was numb.

I had a panic moment, forgetting all about that man on the ground. My thoughts were about Aaron. I needed to get him help, medical attention, maybe even cleanse his wounds with the cold water on the ground until we got aid.

His face would swell if I didn't do something.

Anger.

I was angry.

Seriously? A man dead at my feet and my emotions went to anger?

"Let me get you water. We need to get you to a doctor. Damn that man for doing this to you. I can't believe this…"

"Mom. Stop," Aaron nearly scolded me. "Do you hear yourself?"

"What? Yes. Of course, Aaron your poor face."

"The man, Mom," Aaron said. "We need to get him help."

As I reached out to Aaron, I completely and utterly froze.

It hit me. Gone was the anger.

My eyes slowly cased down to the man. The bloody water spread wider.

"Oh my God." I looked at him. The color had already drained from his face. "Oh my God." I crouched down to him, reaching out my hand. "Wake up. Hey." I nudged him. "Hey."

But I knew. I knew long before that moment, the man was dead.

One would think at that second, that realization would bring guilt…but no.

I was wrought with confusion about what to do.

"Aaron?" I looked up at him. "He's dead."

"He can't be."

"He is," I said.

"What do we do?"

"I did this." I stood up. "I did this. Oh my God. I killed him."

It didn't sink in. Even though my words and actions made it sound like it did, it didn't. Not entirely.

My body started to shake. Not out of remorse. Not out of guilt, but of fear of what would happen to me.

How selfish was that?

I couldn't even absorb any bad feelings. That man and his people stole our car, our food and pummeled my son.

What the hell was wrong with me?

I stepped back away from the body, looking to my right and at the empty streets, then to my left, a mere block away from people and police.

Did anyone see?

Did anyone care?

I may not have felt bad or remorse, but I still knew I had to do the right thing.

Surely, they would see it was self-defense?

Then again, at any point, once the man was down, I could and should have stopped kicking him.

I could have.

I didn't.

I wasn't even sure how many blows I delivered; I had lost it.

"Let's go," I said, reaching out and grabbing Aaron's arm.

"Where?" he asked.

"I have to tell the police what I did. I have to get you help."

"I don't need help."

"I still need to tell the police."

"Mom, they'll arrest you."

"Then they'll arrest me. I…took a life."

There.

There it was.

The moment I spoke those words it hit me. Like a bad dream I was drowning in this instantaneous feeling of dread and guilt.

My mind spun.

My children. Aaron and Cleo. They'd have to go south without me. Would they even evacuate prisoners? Because that's what I would be, a prisoner.

My son pleaded with me to think about what I was doing.

"Please, Mom," he said. "Let's go home. Let's talk to dad. He'll take you. Don't do this now."

No. That wasn't right. I had to do the right thing. As horrible an act as I committed, I couldn't walk away.

What was I thinking when I took this man's life?

I was vicious, out of control.

I wasn't thinking at all.

Just like I wasn't thinking when I walked back toward the police.

I envisioned in my mind I would approach them. I would tell them, "My son and I were attacked, our food was stolen, our car was stolen, a man was beating my son and I killed him."

After saying that, surely, they'd rush to find out more, make a radio call and arrest me.

That wasn't how it went.

"Excuse me, officer." I approached the first one. "My son and I…"

"I can't help you," he said. "Back up."

He didn't even look at me.

I approached another. He at least looked at me and my son.

"My son and I were attacked…"

"Ma'am. Mercy is still taking patients. You both look like you need medical attention. It's about eight blocks away…"

"But I…"

"Sorry," he said and then turned to another person, moving them back, doing his crowd control.

"See, Mom," Aaron said. "We need to go. Now. Forget it."

"What?" I spun to my son. "I can't forget it."

I found another officer and there wasn't going to be any beating around the bush, no starting out about our attack, giving them the opportunity not to listen to us.

I grabbed the next police officer I saw, clutched his arm and said, "I just killed a man."

He was dealing with someone that was yelling, trying to break through the lines. The officer stopped and looked at me.

"What was that?" he asked.

"I just killed a man." I pointed. "Down the street. He's there. He's dead."

His eyes shifted from me to Aaron. "What happened to your faces?"

"We were attacked," I said, then cringed. There I was using that again.

"I see that," he said. "This man you killed…did he do this to you?"

"To my son," I said. "His friends stole my car, our food. He was going after my son, I don't know what happened, I…beat him."

"You…you beat him?" the officer asked. "You beat a man to death?" he asked with a sense of disbelief.

I nodded.

He was going to say something else, but then he was distracted by the crowd. He dealt with them for a few seconds and returned his attention to us. "Lady, I'm going to be honest with you. I can't deal with this right now. Go. Get medical attention and call this in. None of us right now can deal with this."

Was he serious?

Of course he was. He didn't even want to be bothered.

I quit trying to get through to the officers doing crowd control, but I didn't give up.

Walking back to the man, I pulled my phone from my purse and called 911.

It took three attempts and finally I got an answer.

I reported it. I told them where we were and even added that my son needed medical attention. I made the call. The operator told us to stay put.

We did.

My phone died not long after and Aaron hadn't even brought his.

On the street next to the man's body, we stood. Each minute that passed we grew colder and more anxious.

The man lay on the ground, his color had all but drained, slushy water nearly burying his face. People walked by, they looked, but no one stopped.

A police car even raced by…nothing.

I finally started to feel pity for this man.

Did he have family? Did the man and the woman with him even care enough to worry about what had happened to him?

The crowd by the grocery store dwindled and dispersed when the store shut off the lights and closed down. The police presence was still there, but none of them came our way.

As sad as it was, when it started to get dark and I estimated two hours had passed since I made that call…I decided we had to go.

Was it that no one cared or that they simply had other things more pressing to worry about?

I had alerted the authorities, even gave my name. They knew who I was and where to find me.

But I didn't know who the man was. The man whose life I took.

I reached down and felt his pockets, finding his wallet. I pulled it out and looked at his license.

Edward Winfrey. He was forty-two years old and lived not far from our house.

I held on to the wallet and would give it to the authorities when they finally came for me, and they would.

I was ready to face my consequences.

There had to be consequences, right? We were still a civilized world?

Or were we?

It was snowing steadily, the temperature was dropping fast, and we had three miles to walk to get home.

Aaron and I walked mostly in silence.

Walked on an August day in the bitter cold.

The darker it grew, the colder it grew and the quieter it became. The less cars on the road, the less people we saw.

It was evident to me that it was more important to protect commodities, keep the peace and to save lives then to worry about lives lost.

It had only been a couple weeks since everything started and already, we as human beings were changing.

We had become as cold as the weather.

This was only the beginning.

SEVEN

REAL HOME

The only part of my body that didn't feel frozen were my cheeks. It didn't hurt, the pelt icy snow helped with that, but it throbbed. I could only imagine how my son felt. He didn't complain. For the most part, our walk was silent. Unspoken words about an unspeakable act.

Waking three miles wasn't an issue, I had done so before when I was on my fitness kick. Walking every evening at the park until my fitness band said it was three miles. I never really enjoyed it. A lot of people do enjoy the physical energy and the excitement of feeling and looking better. Not me—I'd rather binge-watch Netflix and have a Ho Ho.

Bottom line, I thought I could handle three miles.

However, walking that distance around a park while listening to music was a whole different ballgame than walking the same distance in a bizarre weather system.

I hadn't been out after dark for weeks, not since everything changed. I'd heard stories about how the temperatures plummeted when the sun went down, but I didn't realize until I was out in it.

The wet slush increasingly grew harder and instead of sloshing through, we crunch our way. By the time we neared the house, it was almost impossible to walk.

Had it not been so cold I would have taken off my boots and walked the remaining mile in my socks. That was a trick Helen taught me years before. So I wouldn't 'break a hip' she'd say.

She was right.

The cotton of the socks would stick to the ice allowing me to walk without slipping.

I needed that on the way home, but opted to wait until that final grade leading up to our street. Off went those red rubber boots and cold or not, snow or not, I walked that last ten minutes on the ice in my socks, boots in my hands.

They were damp and stiff by the time I dragged my way to the front door.

The brightness from my home was a guiding light, and the front door flung open before we were halfway up the walk.

Helen and Cleo stood there; they looked like they were ready to come out.

I held up my hand. "No. Don't. It's all ice."

"We were so worried," Helen said, then looked down to Cleo. "Go call Dad and tell him they're home."

My daughter darted from sight.

Finally, we made it to the house and Helen pulled us in, closing the door immediately.

"Oh my God, what happened?" She reached for my coat.

The boots slipped from my hand and landed with a thump in the hall. "More than you want to know."

"I'll go get you guys some blankets." She took a few steps and stopped. "And the first aid kit."

We both stood there in the entrance hallway just staring at each other. Not wanting to say anything. Cleo raced to me hugging my legs.

"Baby, Mommy's wet."

"And cold," she said.

"Yes, and cold."

Aaron removed his coat and hung it on the railing of the stairs by mine. I held the wall for support and removed my socks. My toes were so cold they stung. I didn't want to look at them for fear I'd see frost bite.

As I dropped my last sock, that was when I heard the television. Something about "…images you are seeing…" sounded important and drew my attention.

I took a step toward the living room and all I could see on the television was a city. It was snowing and a reporter stood with her hand out as if trying to catch the flakes while she said something.

Helen returned with a blanket. "Here," she said, placing it over my shoulders. I assumed she had gotten one for Aaron, too.

"I made soup," Helen said. "Come into the kitchen. Let me clean your cuts."

Instead of following her, I murmured a, "Thank you," and, holding the blanket tight to me, walked into the living room.

"And as you can tell, the snow…" the reporter said, "is showing no signs of stopping."

It was at that second I didn't need to hear what city it was, I could tell.

New York.

"How much water are they saying now?" the anchorman asked.

"Right about three feet and growing. But that same water is frozen and they are expecting this snow to get heavier and not let up.

Which will make travel even more dangerous and difficult. Many areas not scheduled for relocation are being moved in an emergency evacuation by bus and other means."

"What the hell?"

"Mac," Helen called my name.

I turned my head to her. "Did you see this?" I asked.

"I've been watching it all night. This is the third city now." She handed me a cup of coffee. "I'm going to clean up Aaron, then you. Okay?"

"Third city?"

"They're saying the snow is falling about half a foot an hour. But they're colder than us."

"Are they saying anything about us?" I asked.

Helen shook her head. "No. Nothing."

For a moment, a brief moment, mesmerized by the news I pushed the events of the day to the back of my mind.

I listened to them talk about snow, evacuations, and dangers to areas in the belt. When they showed that belt, our town was there.

I pulled my daughter closer to me to listen. I had dismissed it from the beginning, always believing nothing would happen, that the freak weather would stop and we'd return to normal.

Now the normal was the prospect of being nomads, moved to a strange city, no home and very few belongings.

I hoped that what happened earlier, acts done by others and myself were a product of fear and panic. Because if they weren't, if they were a sign of things to come, there was absolutely nothing bright about our future.

The warm brandy felt amazing after sipping it. It rolled and warmed my chest with each swallow.

A hot shot, antibiotic cream, and the drink did wonders for making me feel better.

I stood in the dining room staring out the patio doors, watching whatever it could be called fall steadily. It was a mixture of snow, rain and ice.

My mind would drift to the man, wondering if he was still laying there. I gave my name, would the police come for me?

More than likely not on this night.

"He should see a doctor," Glen said as he joined me in the dining room. "Do you need another drink?"

"Yeah, I'll get it though. Can we take him tomorrow?"

"We should. His eye is bad."

I nodded sadly.

Glen stepped to me and looked at my face. "What happened to you guys? Aaron said you were robbed."

"Yeah, we were. The place was insane, mobs were there, arguing, screaming. They took my car, our food, that's why we walked. They attacked me, but Aaron took the brunt of it when he tried to help."

"Did you call the police?"

"Yeah, we did." I finished my brandy and walked towards the cabinet to get another. "Didn't do any good. We went to them and even called." I poured another.

"At least you are okay."

I huffed a sarcastic chuckle.

"What's that's supposed to mean?" Glen questioned. "Are you hurt more than you're telling me?"

I shook my head. "Glen…something…something happened today."

"Like what?" Glen asked. "What else happened?"

I sighed, taking a moment. "When Aaron was getting beaten. I went after the guy."

"Okay."

"I was driven to protect him."

"Of course."

"You would do the same thing, right?" I asked.

"Absolutely. I'd go after the guy."

"Which I did."

"So that's it?" Glen asked.

"I kicked him, you know, and it was the right spot on the leg. He went down. I've never kicked anyone like that before. Hell, I don't think I've ever kicked anyone ever. But your mom's red boots had that steel toe for weight."

Glen nodded listening. "Okay, you kicked him. Good for you."

A huge weight felt lifted from me at that second—he wasn't judging, and that made me happy. I mean, why would my husband judge me?

"It's okay." He reached squeezing my arms, then leaned in and placed his lips to my forehead.

"Then I kicked him again."

Glen froze. Lips not moving. He didn't move.

"And again. And again. I don't know how many times," I said, dazed. "But enough, that when I finally stopped. When I finally snapped out of it…he was dead."

He stepped back. "Jesus, Mac."

"I don't know how I did it."

"Are you sure?"

"Yes. His head was bleeding really—"

"I get it." Glen held up his hand. "What did you do? Did you go find help?"

"I wanted to find help for Aaron…"

"I mean that man," Glen said.

"He was dead."

"And you did nothing?"

"Why does it sound like you're judging me?"

"Really?" Glen laughed once sarcastically. "Mac, you killed a man."

"He was hurting our son."

"You said he was down."

"But for how long?" I defended.

"So you just killed him?"

"No! Not on purpose."

"Only after kicking him over and over."

"Fuck you, Glen, he was hurting our child. What did you expect me to do?"

"Maybe stop when you saw he was hurt."

"I didn't see. I didn't care." I folded my arms.

"Oh my God. You just walked away?"

"No, I didn't. I tried to get the police. They were right there," I said. "They didn't come. One officer told me to call it in which I did. I waited."

"And you left."

"It was cold and dark. Yes, I left. I gave my name."

"You just put our entire family's evacuation in jeopardy because you broke the law."

"Don't be ridiculous I don't think there are laws."

"Oh, stop. There is still law and order."

"No, Glen," I argued. "If there was any semblance of law and order none of this would have happened. People are out there committing crimes and they don't care."

He just stared at me.

"What?"

"Do you?" Glen asked. "Do you care that you did this?"

"I was scared at first, then maybe I felt bad…"

"Maybe?"

"Maybe."

"You don't care what you did, do you?" He asked.

"I care about what I did. I hated what I did. Do I care about the man?" I shook my head. "No."

"When the world falls apart, and you ask what happened to humanity, you'll just need to look in the mirror." He started to leave.

"What the hell is that!" I blasted. "When did you become the righteous carpenter? That was our son. Our son."

Glen walked away and out of the dining room.

I grunted tossing out my hand, swinging at the air in my frustration.

Was my husband really taking that stand with me? Was he really upset?

Perhaps I wasn't gauging the situation right. Maybe I didn't have it in true perspective. I was injured, traumatized and a little numb from the booze. I downed the remainder of my brandy and lifted the bottle. When I did, I saw Helen standing there, waiting for her chance to pounce. "What?" I asked, pouring some. "I'm sure you heard. You want to judge, too?"

"Yes," she said, walking toward me. "That was his child that was hurt and attacked. My grandson. So…my son was an asshole." She grabbed a glass from the tray, and the bottle from my hand. "And you were, too." She poured a splash of brandy in her glass. "I would never have called the cops. That man attacked you and your son. I would have just left him there on the street and wouldn't give it a second thought. That's just me." She shrugged. "I'm a survivor." She brought the glass to her lips and sipped. "Something we all should be right now."

EIGHT

PREP

August 2

My sleep was interrupted three times.

Once to vomit and twice thanks to the loud cracks of thunder. I opened my eyes to see the lightning so severe it flashed like a strobe light in my room while the rain smacked violently against the window.

It only kept me up a few moments. Using the sound of the storm, I fell back to sleep easily.

Then Glen woke me.

The house was cold. It was reminiscent of when it all began.

I started feeling the pain of my cheek and when I lifted my head, I was stuck to the pillow. My wound had bled and clotted against the cotton fabric.

"You need to get up," Glen said. He flicked on the dim light next to my bed.

"What time is it?" I asked.

"A little after nine."

I cringed knowing I had to lift my head and tear my face from the pillow. I hadn't been sleeping too long, but long enough that I was rested. I'd spent the night watching the news, watching the northern coastal cities evacuate.

It was a nightmare and unreal.

How could this be happening? Didn't anyone see it coming?

I watched report after report that the weather was just going to get worse while I drank myself into a state, then stumbled to bed and experienced the dreaded spins.

It was bad and I ended up throwing up. That didn't help. I had to pass out and I did.

My head throbbed. I needed water.

Cringing, I pulled my face from the pillow as I sat up. I immediately felt it bleed and I reached for a tissue next to my bed.

"Mom made coffee," Glen said. "If you want to shower, I suggest you do it now. I don't know how long the power will last."

He still felt off to me. He'd gone to bed without speaking a word to me. A mere kiss to my cheek, not even a goodnight.

I was trying to process why he was so angry.

Granted, my actions were horrendous but weren't they justified?

We were at an impasse over it.

"What's going on?" I asked. "Why are we rushing?"

"We're leaving," he said.

"To take Aaron to the doctor?"

"There's no time for that," he replied. "We're leaving home. We're evacuating."

Helen was being suspiciously nice to me. Maybe she felt bad, I didn't know. She brought me a large mug of coffee and told me, "I would give you a bottle of water, but we need it."

I nodded a thanks as if I understood what was going on. The truth was, I didn't. I was sore, half awake and definitely hungover.

I downed a couple of ibuprofen, had a few swigs of coffee, and turned on the shower, allowing the water to get steaming hot.

I finally…sober…looked in the mirror at my face. My cheek was blue, early bruising and slightly puffy. Dried blood formed a circle from the small cut that was center of the bruise.

I jumped in the shower and it helped a lot. My body and mind felt better. Enough that I was able to look out the window to see what was going on.

We didn't have snow, but the icy rain fell with a vengeance and the wind blew hard, causing waves in the pool.

It was worse than the day before.

Every day was getting worse.

After dressing, I went down to join the family. They were in the kitchen, sitting around the breakfast island, as if waiting on me.

Aaron's poor face was swollen and nearly unrecognizable. It broke my heart to see the bruising and cuts. I ran my hand over his head kissing him on the cheek, then I kissed my daughter.

I poured myself some more coffee to warm what was in my mug and that was when the lights went out. My eyes looked to the ceiling.

"We don't have a lot of time," Glen said. "Please sit down."

"Did they up our evacuation?" I asked. "Change it?"

"No," Glen replied. "We're not waiting on that."

"But our destination isn't done. It was under construction."

"We're heading to Uncle Fred's," Helen answered. "It's not far from our relocation."

"I don't understand," I said. "We're leaving when we're not supposed to. Glen, they have the roads monitored. We won't get through."

"The main roads."

I huffed a ridiculed laugh. "Those are the safe roads."

"We have to take our chances," Glen said. "Have you seen it out there? It's bad and getting worse. They are evacuating Philly today." His finger tapped hard on the counter. "Right now. We're fifty miles from Philly. We have to leave soon. I don't want to chance being stuck here if this weather gets any worse. And it will. Our best bet is to leave right now, cram into my truck, not to get caught in the traffic of the exodus, take the back roads and get to Uncle Fred's."

I brought my coffee to my lips and simply nodded.

"Everyone is allowed a backpack," Glen said. "Not that it matters as we're avoiding the checkpoints. But I have been up since dawn. Everyone's pack has three days' rations, a couple bottles of water, and a change of clothes."

"Socks, too," said Helen. "Everyone has extra socks. One pair are in a plastic bag and you are not to use them."

"Is this what you got from the man?" Aaron asked.

Man? What man?

"Yes," Glen answered.

"What are we talking about?" I asked.

"The man on the TV was telling people what to put in their personal bag. I did the best I could to follow. Cleo's will be heavy, we'll carry it."

It was obvious all of them had been up longer than me and had discussed things. I was lost.

"Why are we carrying anything?" I asked.

"Hopefully, we won't have to," Glen replied. "But the guy on the news, he's some sort of prepper expert. He said to pack the personal bag, the backpack, as if you have to end up walking."

"The socks," Helen added. "Everyone should wear three pairs. The one in the plastic baggy is if we do walk, you can take off the cold wet ones and switch them out."

"You want to take the back roads," I said. "They can't be safe. Wouldn't it be safer if we wait for our time to go? Take the route they will have cleared for us?"

"No," Glen answered. "If we wait two things will happen. There's no power, we'll freeze. And second, we'll not be able to get out…and we'll die."

The whole thing seemed over the top. Rushing to leave. If the government was telling us about evacuation, wouldn't they have us covered? Wouldn't they have us leave before things got too bad? And freeze to death? I thought Glen was exaggerating. The power went out all the time. Rolling blackouts, did he forget about them?

But I didn't have a chance. He and my mother-in-law had my family in a 'flight for life' mode and I had no choice but to go along with it.

<><><><>

The airline-style rules of one bag, one personal belonging, and one duffle applied to when refugees checked into their evacuation camp. We weren't heading to our camp, we were headed to Uncle Fred's, so I didn't understand why I had to leave so much behind.

If I would have had one more hour, one more bag, there was so much I would have taken. Nothing big, but pieces of my life I was being forced to leave behind.

Glen explained that if we had to stop, walk, and go to a camp, then we'd have to leave things behind anyways. It was better to prepare for a camp and not go, then not prepare and end up in one.

We were leaving before our evacuation time. Weeks earlier, in fact. I didn't think anyone else would rush to run for the hills, or rather south, like we were.

I was wrong.

The major routes were definitely out: they checked for evacuation dates.

Traffic crawled out of our small town at a snail's pace, but traffic wasn't the reason we moved slowly. The weather was. It was relentless. The storms continued, and the winds seemed to blow at hurricane strengths.

At least from my perspective.

I stayed in the back seat of the truck with the kids, Cleo in the middle and Aaron behind Helen, who rode up front with Glen. It was best that way. It was too cramped for Helen, and Glen wasn't exactly talking very much to me. I guess in his mind his wife was a cold-blooded killer.

In a sense I was, but I knew in my heart, even though I was unable to control what I did, I was justified.

Once out of Allentown, we hopped on 145 which would take us to Route 309. The 145 moved steadily about twenty-five miles an hour, but 309 was jam-packed. No one would let us on, traffic was backed up on the entranceway and we sat there for an hour, inching our way.

Eventually, Glen pulled off to take even more secondary roads.

The goal was to get south and avoid crossing water as much as possible. That was easier said than done. The rivers, streams and lakes were high and the weather made them violent.

That was what we'd heard on the news before we lost all power.

Everywhere lost power all at once. There wasn't even a radio station we could reach. We were on our own as far as information went.

At the rate we were moving and the long route we were taking it would take us over twenty-four hours to get to Fred's.

The kids were hungry, but we couldn't feed them. We had to conserve food and it wasn't like we could stop and get a take-out burger. Nowhere was open.

Soon enough, we would run into cars that had run out of fuel. With the rate of detours and road closures, it was possible most Pennsylvanians would run out of gas before they left their home state.

We were lucky. Glenn's compensation of fuel was strapped in containers in the back of the truck.

We were moving steadily until another road closure took us slightly east and through the town of Pennsburg.

Pennsburg was a ghost town when we arrived. No one walked the streets; the shops and houses were dark; the only life we saw was the stream of cars that followed Leyfield Road through the town.

The weather seemed especially volatile, which made sense because we were near a body of water.

Water we had to cross.

Leyfield Road rested on what I would call a natural bridge over Green Lane Water reserve. A road built on a strip of land that bridged the water. A three-hundred-foot section at the end was the only manmade portion.

Crossing that water had to be one of the scariest experiences of my life. I didn't know how high the bridge was supposed to be above the water, but at that point, with all the rain, it was nearly flush.

In the barely moving line of cars, water careened over the bridge, smacking into cars, not hard enough to move any, but it carried debris that caused damage to vehicles.

I watched a tree smash into an SUV. He was in the lane next to us and two car lengths ahead.

The driver stepped out of the car but then reached back inside.

"What is he doing?" Glen spoke, then hit the horn. "He needs to get back in."

"Maybe his car won't drive," Helen suggested.

"No, he can drive it over this bridge. He cannot block traffic." Glen laid on the horn again. "Come on, buddy! Do that off the bridge!" He honked again.

"Glen," I said. "Beeping at him isn't going to work. Maybe he's hurt."

"So says the humanitarian," Glen snapped.

"Fuck you."

"No, fuck you."

"Hey!" Helen blasted. "Enough. Just…worry about us, Glen, okay. We'll be off this bridge before we know it."

It couldn't be soon enough.

Every splash and crash of water hitting against our truck had me praying that Glen's karma wouldn't strike us.

As we crept passed the man, he was distraught, screaming and crying, hands on his head as he stared inside his vehicle.

The tree limb had made it inside his car and I quickly covered Cleo's eye when we drove past and saw it had impaled the female in the front passenger's seat.

Once we had made it across, I heaved out a huge breath of relief. It was the last bridge for a while…or so we thought.

Immediately, there was another 'road closed' sign and we had to follow the traffic. It turned left and over another bridge.

It took forty minutes to cross the first bridge. This one wasn't as big, so shouldn't have taken long. The water and storm were worse, though. More cars were hit with something, water, debris, and we were not immune. Our truck, like every other vehicle, was continuously pelted with something. My eyes stayed locked on the back window watching the water, watching the storm.

In such a daze, my reaction was slow when a tree limb hit right below my window into the small door. I jumped with a scream, grabbing my chest. By the time I caught my bearings, calmed down and returned to looking out the window…I saw it.

"Glen," I called his name with warning.

"I see it."

"Oh my God."

"Mac, I see it we're almost at the end. Almost there," he said.

I leaned in toward Cleo to get a glance out of the windshield. Even with the heavy, rainy ice, I could see we were almost at the end.

Would it be quick enough?

I looked out of my window again. It rolled our way, menacingly making its way to the bridge. It looked like a wave, a big brown wave, but it wasn't. It was a huge mountain of debris. Trees, cars, parts of houses, huge chunks of ice rode the violent current of water that headed our way.

"Hurry," I urged him.

"I can't go any faster."

It rolled closer.

"Glen," I peeped out his name, tensing my body, and grabbing on to Cleo in her booster seat.

I kept watching.

A second after Glen gunned the truck forward with a jerk, the barreling wall of debris slammed into the bridge.

It was like a monster, swallowing everything. A water avalanche, devouring everything in its path and growing bigger.

We had made it somewhat to the end of the bridge. I thought we were in the clear, then the force of the water pushed a car into the tail end of our truck. It sent us into a counterclockwise spin. My body jerked to the left as we rammed into another car then slid until we came to a halt against the rail of the bridge.

The sound of rushing water was frightening, it was so loud. I spun to look out the back window. The bridge was completely gone, and the massive pile of debris was making its way downstream.

"We have to get out. Get out now!" Glen said, putting the truck in gear. "Aaron get the baby out. Mac, grab the back packs."

Aaron wasted no time. He opened his door, grabbed Cleo as soon as I unlatched her buckle and snatched up one of the backpacks.

"Dad, hurry," he shouted.

"Run to the shore!" Glen yelled as he reached down between the front seats and grabbed a bag. He opened his door, shouting as he did, "Come on, let's go."

"Get to the kids," Helen said. "We'll be right there."

I watched as my son, slipping and sliding, ran, but as he made it off the bridge he stopped and stood there.

I was ready and had two packs looped around my arm when I reached for my door.

It wouldn't open.

Helen was out of the truck, and she stood looking in the door. "What's wrong?"

"It's jammed. It won't open." I hit into it, pushing and pushing. "It won't open." In the midst of trying, I raised my eyes to see another wave of debris coming our way. It wasn't as big. Maybe I'd be safe. I lost all reason and flew into a total state of panic, slamming my arm against the door. It hadn't even crossed my mind to try the other door until Helen opened it.

"Here." She calmly leaned into the truck, holding out her hand. "Come on."

Crash!

I'm not sure what exactly happened at that second. I was focused on Helen, reaching for her hand when the truck violently jolted. It happened so fast.

The force of the hit tipped the truck onto the driver's side wheels and Helen fell into the cab. The open rear door slammed and her body rolled across the narrow back seat into me, pinning my face against the door window. Pinned against the glass, I watched as we dropped fast and hard.

We splashed into the muddy water. The truck bounced upward only to be slammed by debris and carried fast and furiously with the rubble-filled current.

There wasn't time to scream or react. It would end eventually. I was convinced it would end with the truck submerging and us drowning in icy cold waters.

I wasn't sure how far down the river we were carried, but it was as if the monstrous wave was done with us and tossed us aside, ass end up and we came to a halt, nose of the truck to the ground at a forty-five degree angle. If I didn't know better, the way we ended up, I would have sworn we went over a ledge or cliff. It was over, we weren't moving anymore.

We made it.

"Helen?"

Helen lifted from me, holding on to the seat.

I quickly looked out of my window, I didn't see any water, then I looked to the front seat. The front end was submerged and the windshield looked as if it pressed against mud.

Carefully, I moved enough to get a better view out my window. "Okay. Okay, we're good. If we get out, we just need to jump. We're close to the shore." I tried my door again. It still wouldn't open. "This is still stuck. Try that door."

Helen nodded and scooted over to the other door. "No water on this side," she said after looking out, then reached for the handle. "Nothing. It's jammed."

"Shit. Maybe if we both push," I suggested.

"We can try," Helen said.

Just as I started to move her way, a huge chunk of ice crashed through the rear cab window, narrowly missing us both. It went between us, straight down and through the windshield.

Thick mud began to seep in.

With the back window broken, it gave us a way out.

I didn't know how steady the truck was, so we had to move fast and carefully. I climbed out first, my coat and gloved hand protecting me from the shards of glass.

As soon as I was out, Helen shoved out the backpacks. "We're gonna need these," she shouted.

I moved the bags to the side, just under the window and gave her my hand to help her out.

I started thinking about Glen and the kids, how mortified they had to have been when they saw us being washed away. How happy they would be to know we were alive. We'd have to go upstream to find them.

"I don't have any idea how far we were carried," I said when Helen's head and shoulders poked through the window. "We'll have to walk."

"I figured," she grunted as she tried to get through.

I purchased a foot hold on the edge of the truck bed as I pulled on her arms to help her through.

Finally, she emerged enough to climb the rest of the way out herself.

"You okay?" I asked.

"Yes, I'm fine." Helen teetered as she stood. "I'm sure I'll feel it tomorrow. But I'm tough."

"You are."

I noticed she was in a frozen state, not moving, just staring.

"Helen?"

"Oh, Mac," she said with sadness. "Oh, Mac."

Instead of asking *what?* I realized she was looking upstream, something I didn't do when I got out.

Finally, I looked. I wished I hadn't.

Everything was different. I couldn't even see the river. Broken trees, parts of homes, automobiles, and ice slowly bounced in the thick muddy water.

There was no longer a landscape, the flash flood had cleared it all, even things on the shore.

I didn't know how far the current had carried us, but I did know everything behind us, the direction we had to go to find our family, was completely and utterly destroyed.

NINE

A BOOT

One canister survived. The lonely, green five-gallon gas tank made it only because one of the bungee cords refused to let go and became hooked on the handle in a freakish save. I unhooked it, lifted it out and placed it on the ground. We would need it. Maybe not for fuel, but definitely bartering.

Maybe our family would need a ride. Obviously since our truck was a goner.

Fortunately, from what I could figure out, we found ourselves on the correct side of the river. The side my family would be on. My eyesight was jaded by the continuous icy rain, but after a squint or two I could make out the river's edge.

I couldn't see the natural bridge or part of the manmade one that had collapsed and sent us into the raging river.

I was ready for the walk, which had to be at least a mile, maybe more. My coat was a good one. It came to my thighs, and was lightweight and warm, but it still was a bulky mess when it came to placing on my backpack. Helen didn't look so loaded down, not as much as I did.

It was so cold, once out of the truck and on to the ground I put on my gloves, then searched my pockets on my coat frantically.

"What?" Helen asked. "What did you lose?"

"My hat. It's okay, though, I have a hood." I lifted my hood which formed more of a tent rather than something tight to my head.

"Wait. Here. Put this on under that hood." She swung her backpack around, reached inside, and pulled out one of those thick plastic rain bonnets. Only the one she offered me had bright yellow flowers. "Aaron got me a six-pack of these."

"Um, no."

"Yes."

"It's plastic. How will it keep me warm?"

"Because it is plastic. Trust me you'll keep the heat in better. Put it on then pull that hood over it," Helen said. "Plus, the visor will keep the rain from your eyes."

After some hesitation, and looking at her as she wore hers, I took it with a, "Fine. Thank you," then placed it on my head, tying it under the chin. I could only imagine how ridiculous I looked, but that didn't matter. Staying warm and dry did.

We moved forward, trampling over debris, bogged down with the backpacks and the heavy gas canister. So much so I had to stop every fifty feet to set it down, shake my arm and lift it again.

If it was possible for slush to fall from the sky, that's what it felt like. A thick, icy rain speckled with ice, like one of those frozen slushy drinks from a convenience store.

I wished I had known Pennsburg enough to recognize something, some way to get a sense of direction. But I recognized nothing, until I spotted it.

The natural bridge that ran across the river was only partially intact, the calamity of refuge had broken through it like a dam. And I could see on our side a piece of the man-made bridge.

The one thing I didn't see...was my family.

"No," I gasped out.

"Don't tell me that was the bridge we were on," Helen said.

I wanted to run there, drop everything and race ahead but a part of me didn't want to see. What was the last thing I remembered? I was stuck. I knew that. Glen went to the children who were off the bridge.

My head was foggy, I was trying to picture the last things I saw.

"Helen, what do you remember? Where were they when we dropped?"

"They ran off the bridge. They were off before we knew you were trapped," Helen said.

"Are we sure?"

"Positive. Aaron had Cleo. He was holding her."

"You're sure?"

"Yes. Positive. They weren't on the bridge. They were with the others that ran. He held her; I can still see them standing there."

That's right. He did run. Glen told them to get to the shore, after Aaron yelled for us to hurry.

"What about Glen?" I asked.

"He was running to them."

"Was?" I asked.

"He stopped. I think he was headed to us." Helen paused. "No. No. I was outside the truck. He saw me getting you. No, he stayed put."

Nervously I nodded in acknowledgement of what she said. My eyes gazed toward the broken bridge and the shore. No one was there. Then again, it was freezing and wet. It had taken us some time to get upstream through that debris. Maybe everyone just left. The only way we would know was to get there and climb up that grade and see for ourselves.

68

If people left, surely there would be a sign.

Once we got close enough, I wasn't sure we'd find anything. It was disheartening and frightening. There was a low-grade, longer climb that led to the road, and a steeper one that led to small sections of the bridge still intact.

What looked like a mound of dirt with objects emerging was on the land below the broken bridge. Were they things that came down in the flash flood from the river? Or had they fallen, like us, from the bridge and road?

A midsize car was at the bottom of the steep slope, that car obviously plunged. One of the doors was open. Apprehensively, I approached it, peeking inside. It was empty. Whoever was in there had gotten out and was long gone.

I took that as a good sign, especially for my family.

The car and the slope, even the remaining section of the bridge, were covered in mud.

Not only had rubble rolled through, some sort of wave of mud had as well and coated everything like thick fudge.

It was twenty feet above us and hard to see if anything or anyone was there. We didn't hear a sound except for the falling rain and the thick dripping, oozing mud.

Helen and I had a choice. We could chance the steep grade or walk the low slope up to the road. Truly, there was no option. We were carrying items and didn't have hands free enough to grab on for leverage. Plus, the moving mud would make the steeper one impossible.

In some parts our feet sunk, getting stuck in the thick substance. Pulling out we had to be careful not to lose our shoes. I wished, as we took that slope, I had one of those rain bonnets for my feet. Helen was right. The only part of my body that was dry and holding in heat was my head.

At last I made it to the top first.

"Stay put," I told Helen, then turned to look for the road.

I could see it where the mud thinned out and ended. I hurried to the road, set down my items where I knew they'd be safe and returned to Helen.

It was harder going back down that slope than up. I slid a lot as I reached down to give her a hand. She accepted my assistance and, finally, we were both safe, out of the river and on solid ground.

Some of the icy water formed small pools, while the rest ran off the sides.

There wasn't a car or person in sight.

"Tracks," Helen said. "Look tracks. Footprints and cars."

"So everyone left," I said.

"They probably took off for safety. This mud may have just come. More than likely this isn't safe."

"Okay. Okay," I replied, somewhat breathlessly. "Where are Glen and the kids?"

"Maybe they went for help for us. They probably saw the truck go down the river."

I nodded. "And they went to look for us?"

"Maybe," Helen said. "I would."

"Me too." Sniffling in once, I turned to look behind me and to the direction of the broken bridge. I took a few steps toward the mud, trying to put myself in Glen's position, trying to recreate in my mind what they may have witnessed.

I stared out at the mud that grew thicker and thicker as it neared the remains of the bridge and that was when I noticed something odd about it.

I wasn't sure what it was, so I walked closer to it.

"Mac?" Helen called to me.

"Stay there, Helen."

"Mac, get back here. That is dangerous. You can see where mud just flashed over like lava. You don't know what's under it."

Keeping my slow, steady pace, I looked over my shoulder and back to Helen. "I know, I just have to…" Something caught my foot and down I went, tripping hands and face first into the mud.

When I landed, the pressure of my fall against the soft mud rippled out the sludgy substance exposing a woman's hand. The perfectly manicured nails were covered with dirt and her fingers curled in a partial fist.

Instinctively, I screamed.

"What is it?"

"Stay back!" I told her. "Oh my God, it's a hand."

I don't know why or what caused me to do it, but I grabbed hold of that hand and pulled on it as I stood.

She was in there good and tight, but I was able to free her arm and eventually her shoulder, but when her body lifted up, she brought with it, the arm of a man.

My eyes widened in horror. "Helen! They're bodies."

"What?"

"There are bodies buried under here. Bodies."

I tried to back up but my foot sunk a little. Even though I didn't see it, I felt my shoe touch something and I knew, that too, was a body.

I grew instantly frantic.

I didn't care that it was dangerous. Where I stood, where the mud rushed over, was exactly the last place I remembered seeing my family.

Dropping to my knees, I sunk my hands purposely into the mud and desperately began moving it around. Feeling and digging. Every few seconds, my hand touched another body. When it did, I uncovered it with fear, hoping it wasn't one of my children.

"Dear, sweet God," Helen called out. "There are so many."

Hands deep in the mud, I turned to look to see Helen doing the same as me. She searched the mud. Neither one of us said why we were doing it. It was just known.

I groaned out painful aches of sadness with each limb, I uncovered.

A woman, a man. I felt a beard. Not Glen.

Another man…too thick.

On my hands and knees I moved fast, pushing and reaching.

"How are there so many," Helen said. "How did this…?"

She stopped speaking.

She'd found something. That would be the only reason she stopped talking.

No. No. No. Please, no.

I scrunched my face, closed my eyes tight for a second to summon the strength, and I looked.

Helen had stood. She moved like a drunk, staggering haplessly to an area not far from where she'd been digging. I watched as she reached down.

"Helen?"

She slowly turned around and faced me. In her hand, she clutched a tiny pink boot.

Even though it was dirty, I could identify it. Thick tan sole, pink boot with fur on the top. The boot, the same exact boot Cleo was wearing,

"It wasn't buried," Helen said. "It was laying on the ground. Maybe it's not hers." With a rush she cleaned it and looked inside. Her face immediately looked drawn. "Size twelve."

My heart sunk to my stomach. Where the boot was found, that was where we needed to look. I jumped up to rush her way, but when I did, the ground beneath my feet gave out and the mound of mud collapsed, taking me with it.

I felt like I was free-falling in slow motion, like a dream, carried slowly in a thick substance, but it was neither soft nor mentally easy because falling with me were the bodies buried in the mud.

The landing wasn't too bad—I ended up on that mound of debris and mud under the bridge. Quickly, I rolled out of the way, but I wasn't fast enough. The body of a woman hit into me sending me face first back into the mud.

I heard Helen calling my name. I coughed as I lifted my head and hollered out, "I'm okay. I'm okay."

Pushing the body of the woman from me, I cringed as I made it to a sloppy stand.

At least a dozen bodies were around me. Toppled on each other. All of them with this shocked look on their faces, dirt and mud seeping from their mouths and noses.

I had to look at them. I had to examine them all. Even if only briefly. I knew there was a chance my family could be there.

As much as it pained me to look, I did. Trying my hardest not to step on a body, I inched my way around, looking at them. The faces, the hands, anything that would dismiss them as my own flesh and blood.

Another step and turn was my next mistake.

I wasn't truly on solid ground like I deceivingly believed.

Everything collapsed and down I went again.

Only this time I plunged into icy waters. I went under and everything closed in above my head. Sealing me in.

My own water tomb.

It was cold, dark and the water was painful. I would have never believed something like water could hurt so badly. It seemed to suck what air I held out of my body.

I tried with all my might to hold my breath and reach for the top. To find my way out. I kept my wits, at least I thought so. It was useless.

My lightweight, winter wonderland coat absorbed the water and became a weight. Every time I believed I grabbed onto something, a branch, a piece of wood, my hands slipped and I went down.

I kicked and kicked, needing to get my head above water, get a breath, but I was losing that battle.

I felt the pain start to leave.

My end was near.

Just fight, I told myself, *just fight until you can't fight anymore.*

Please. Please. Let me get something. One thing. Something I can grab on to.

I desperately reached up one more time.

My hand was grabbed.

It was a firm grip.

Helen.

Oh, God, thank God, Helen.

I could feel the pull of my body and saw the light as the debris was cleared.

It didn't even register to me how strong Helen was. My right arm felt pulled from the socket as she grabbed hold of my jacket, and with one strong yank hoisted me out of the water.

As cold as it was outside, it felt warm the second I emerged from the water.

I gasped and coughed; my vision was blurry. I blinked a couple of times and opened my eyes.

It wasn't Helen that saved me.

It was a man. A stranger.

And I owed him my life.

TEN

RECHARGE

I wanted to say, "I was fine. It's okay," and, "Thank you."

In those after moments of being pulled from the river, my adrenaline pumped and I really didn't feel much of anything except gratefulness.

This stranger, this…man, not only pulled me from the river, but once he had me out, he lifted me and carried me in his arms to solid ground. Which I believe was the small grade Helen and I took to get to the road.

He set me down. "Ma'am, please stay up there," he ordered gently to Helen as he gazed up the slope.

Who was he? Where did he come from?

He wasn't wearing arctic wear or any heavy items like I was. He wore a canvas winter coat, no hat, but he had on gloves.

At that moment I wasn't getting a good look at his face. He faced Helen up on the hill.

His hair was long, jet black, and pulled back into a low ponytail. It was wet from the weather and a few strands dangled down.

His hand rested on my shoulder and he glanced at me. "Can you walk?"

"Yeah, yeah. I think I can."

He placed his hand under my arm and helped me to stand. As soon as I stood, my legs felt like jelly, as if I'd just run a marathon.

"Alright, you're not walking anywhere. Just stay here," he said. "I need you to get out of those wet clothes."

"I don't feel cold," I said. "Just numb from the water."

"That's hypothermia. Take them off. Everything. You can leave the uh…plastic hat on."

I reached up—it was still on my head.

"Do you need help?" he asked.

"No, I think I can…"

"I'll be right back." He stood. "Off," he said with a point of his finger and moved up the hill.

I honestly felt fine. I was cold and expected to be shivering out of control, but I wasn't. Everything on me was soaked and stiffening quickly.

I removed my gloves and set them aside on the ground next to me. I could feel the hood of my coat was heavy with water. My fingers couldn't feel a thing, even the zipper on my coat. I had absolutely no feeling whatsoever in them. I fumbled and found the zipper, pulling it down and removed my coat.

My clothes underneath were soaked as well. Two tee shirts and a sweater. They were easy to take off. My boots and socks as well.

I thought of that extra pair of socks in a plastic bag and how they would be welcome.

My blue jeans, however, were a different story. I struggled with them. I even tried to stand again to remove them. They weren't that tight on me, they'd just started to freeze. As I pushed to roll them off, I felt a blanket go over my shoulders and head.

He had returned.

"Let me help you," he said.

"No, I…" I grunted as I pushed the jeans to my hips.

"I got it." He grabbed hold of the fabric by the calves. "Hold on."

First thought I had was *hold on to what?* but I clutched what I could in the muddy ground with my bare fingers and he pulled the wet garment from me.

He wrapped the blanket around me tighter, then lifted me from the ground and carried me up the slope to the top.

I expected him to set me down, but he didn't. He kept carrying me, taking me to an old white pickup truck. The truck was running and the steam from the tail pipe blasted out.

He opened the passenger door and placed me inside. "I'll be back. I'll get your things." And he closed the door.

Helen was in the truck, seated in the middle. She immediately grabbed a hold of me. "Thank God you're alright. Thank God." She pulled me closer and adjusted the vents in the truck to blow warm air on me.

"I'm fine, I think."

Helen's hands moved up and down on my arms in a motherly way, trying to warm me.

"Who is he?" I asked.

"I don't know. But he saved your life."

"I know. Where did he come from?"

"He pulled up as soon as you went down and…" She stopped speaking at the thump sound from the back of the truck. We both looked back.

He was dropping things in and then secured a tarp.

He looked tall, well over six feet with what looked like a strong build, but it was hard to tell with the coat he wore. But he had to be strong the way he just pulled me from the water. He was what I would describe age wise as a man. Not young, not old, maybe in his late forties.

After securing the tarp, he got in the tuck, in the driver's seat, took a breath, cleared his wet strands of hair from his face and grabbed the wheel.

"Hey," I said softly, catching my breath. "Thank you." The words shook as I said them. "Thank you so much."

"You're welcome," he replied.

"How…how did you get such impeccable timing?" I asked.

"Are you shivering?" he questioned.

"Huh?" His lack of answer and change of subject took me by surprise. "Um, yes, I am. I just started."

"She's cold," Helen said.

"That's a good thing. She's warming. She needs to be warmer."

When I saw him reach for the gear, I called out, "Wait. Wait."

"What?" he asked.

"Where are you going? Where are you taking us? For help?"

"There's no help. Not right now. It'll be dark soon," he replied. "We need to get shelter for the night. There's no power. The weather will make it hard to see."

"My family…our family was on this road. By the bridge. I have to keep looking," I told him as I felt Helen clutch my hand. "I need to know. I need to look at the bodies."

"There were a lot of people that made if off the bridge," he said. "They were taken to a transport on the evacuation route."

"The 476?" Helen asked.

He nodded. "Yes."

"That's closed to anyone not on the schedule to leave," she said.

"That's where they went," he said.

"How do you know?" Helen asked.

"I took ten people," he replied. "I came back to see if anyone else was here. I pulled up at the right time I guess."

"You did," I replied. "And I am so grateful. But I can't go anywhere."

"I don't have the fuel to run this truck all night to keep you warm," he said. "You need to get warm. You need shelter. You're still in danger, health wise."

"I can't leave here."

"Can I ask why you believe they are back there?" he questioned.

"They were standing near there when our truck went down," I said.

"Your truck went down?" he asked. "What do you mean?"

Helen answered, "We were on the bridge, the part that broke. My son Glen had gotten across the bridge with the children before he realized Mac was stuck. I was getting her out of the truck when it collapsed."

"They were right there at the edge," I said. "The last I looked."

"I had no idea," he said. "I thought you two were just walking. So your truck went into the river when the bridge went down, when the flood hit. You were carried downstream and walked all the way back here?" he asked.

"Yes," I replied. "We did."

"The bridge collapsed over two hours ago. I was in the traffic ahead of the collapse and flood. Everybody's long gone. I've made two trips."

"Taking people?" I asked. "So you may have seen them. My husband is tall, thin, he was wearing a knit Eagles cap. He would have been with a teenage boy and a little girl."

"I'm sorry," he said. "I took no one like that. A lot of strangers in cars took people with them."

My head dropped. "All the more reason I can't leave."

"Because I didn't see them doesn't mean they didn't leave. There was a lot of hysteria. Maybe…and this is my thinking," he said. "Don't look to the back, look forward. Instead of believing your family is with those bodies, believe your family is with the transport. Or in a car with a stranger who helped them. Instead of believing them dead, believe them to be alive. Instead of looking for their bodies…look for them instead."

His words were impacting and emotionally humbling.

We were quiet for a few seconds. Helen gave me another embrace, then removed her arm and tapped the stranger on the hand.

"Go on," she told him. "Thank you for everything. We're ready."

When she said that, I noticed the pink boot on her lap. I reached for it and she handed it to me as we started to drive.

I knew and felt without a shadow of a doubt that it was Cleo's. But like the stranger suggested, I had to believe she lost that boot when fleeing, instead of losing it while being buried.

I clutched that boot close to my chest as I clutched onto the hope that she, my son, and husband were still alive and out there.

ELEVEN

COLLECTIVE

The saving stranger took off his coat while he drove, then Helen unzipped hers and even removed the plastic bonnet. I guess they were warm. Me, I was still cold and supposed I'd be for a while.

We moved down the road, the tires cutting through the slush. It was coming down steadily; a coat instantly formed on the windshield and the wipers cleared it with each swipe. He slowed down once the road turned residential. Houses, spread apart, lined both sides of the road. They were dark—I didn't see any movement or lights.

He dropped his speed to a turtle's pace, looking from the windshield to his window.

"Is it that bad?" I asked.

"Excuse me?" he replied.

"You really dropped the speed, are the roads that bad?"

"No." He shook his head. "It's not bad out."

"Not bad?" Helen asked with laugh.

"Not to me," he said. "I'm from Saskatchewan. This isn't bad to me at all. I'll let you know when I think it's bad."

I nodded slowly. 'So, then why are we driving so slow?"

"Why are you questioning the man?" Helen defended.

"I'm just wondering."

"I'm driving slow," he said, "because I'm looking for a house for us to stop for the evening."

"They all look empty to me," Helen commented.

"Now who's questioning him," I said.

"I am looking for something specific," he told us. "I'm looking at the chimneys."

"A fireplace," I said.

"Yes." He nodded. "You can tell a fireplace chimney, but more so we need to look for one that has been used. It'll be marked on top. And..." He pointed to the brown brick home half a block away, set back from the road.

"Are you sure?" Helen asked.

"Yes, pretty sure. We'll find out." He turned left and into the driveway, pulling nearly all the way to the garage. "Stay here. I will check out the house." He put his coat back on, opened the truck door and got out.

We watched as he walked to the house and knocked on the door. He waited a few seconds then knocked again. He tried the knob and looked into windows, then he walked around.

"You think he's breaking in?" Helen asked.

"Probably."

"Hmm." She looked at me. "How are you feeling?"

"Cold. A little weak."

"You could have died."

"I know. I wasn't trying to."

"You just went straight down," Helen said. "That was scary. I'm surprised you aren't in pain."

"Probably will be once I stop being cold."

"Probably." Helen stared at the house. "I wonder if he got in?"

"More than likely."

"We don't even know his name, you know."

"You didn't get it?" I asked.

Helen shook her head. "No. I didn't ask. I guess that's rude. We lucked out, though. He's from Canada. This weather is probably nothing for him."

"They were saying on the news a lot of Canadians didn't want to evacuate."

"They probably think we're all overreacting," she said. "You know how we used to make fun of the people in Georgia when they would close schools over a dusting."

"He's probably thinking we have no idea what 'bad snow' really is. I mean, we are just running south because they said to. If this is the worst of it, we could have stayed put."

"Not so sure it would be all that easy without power. We've become a pretty complacent society with technology." She looked back at the house. "I wonder what's taking him so long. I hope he wasn't killed."

"What do you mean?"

"I mean, what if he broke in there and someone was waiting with a gun and shot him. That would suck."

"Yeah, it would. And we're just sitting here."

What else could we do?

We waited, watching the house. I debated in my mind if we should go in there. Then, finally, he came through the front door and walked to the truck.

"Okay," he said, then reached in and shut off the ignition. "House is empty. They were using the fireplace before they left. I got a fire going. There isn't much wood there, but enough for the night. Let's go in."

I didn't have any shoes on so I was at his mercy to help me into the house.

The house felt cold, but once in the back family room, where the fire brewed in the fireplace, it was warmer.

He had brought in our bags from the truck. My clothes were in there and the pair of socks in the plastic bag were heaven. But my layers of clothes were still soaking wet. I doubted they would be dry by morning. My coat would. The light airiness would help it dry faster and I turned it every fifteen minutes as it lay before the fire.

The house wasn't big. I guessed a three bedroom with an addition. It was somewhat disorganized, cabinets open, things knocked over and items scattered about.

The occupants had left in a hurry. The people that lived in the house must have been out of power for a few days. They had been using the fireplace, even tossing a grate over it for cooking.

They left food behind. Not much, no one really had much. Enough for Helen to make a meal meaning we didn't have to use what we had in our packs. In fact, we probably would take the remaining cans from the house. In the freezer, she found two filet mignon steaks. They were still partially frozen, so were still good. She cut them up and using a couple things from the cabinet, tossed it in a pot and in the fire.

They left a lot of things behind. Of course, the one bag evacuation law helped with that. While supper cooked, I sat by the fireplace in a partially laying down position, while Helen and the man went through the house.

She found me some clothes that I could layer and a new knit cap. I took the knit cap, but that damn plastic bonnet kept my head warm and dry and the brandy Helen stashed in her backpack, kept my chest warm as I sipped it.

85

"I found another bottle upstairs," Helen said as she checked her concoction. "Something tells me once we get to that camp, there won't be any bottles."

"Maybe if we go out scavenging we'll find some," I said.

"Maybe. I would say Fred has some, but he probably already killed his stash." She clicked the spoon on the side of the pot and looked up when he walked in the room. "Just in time. Supper's done. Can I get you to get the pot out of the fireplace? Put it on the towel." She handed him the oven mitts and stood up, walking toward the kitchen.

"Smells good," he said, lifting the pot from the fire.

"Helen is a good cook. I'll give her that."

"Your mother...in law?" he asked as if guessing.

"She is. I guess she is more of a mother than I ever really wanted to admit."

"Aw," Helen said as she returned to the room. "I think that's the nicest thing you've said about me." She crouched down to the floor, in her hands were three bowls and silverware. "But I knew that." She grabbed the serving spoon, placed a helping in a bowl and gave it to him. "By now you know my name is Helen. In case you're wondering, and I know you are, her name is Mackenzie. We call her Mac."

"Thank you," he said accepting his bowl of stew and fork. "I figured her name was Mac. I'm Don."

Helen paused. "Don?" She placed a serving in a bowl and handed it to me. "Just Don? Is that your given name? Nothing longer? Just Don?"

"Ald," he said. "As in Donald."

"And your last name?" she asked.

"Johnson."

"Like the actor?" she said.

"Only I'm better looking."

"I'll give you that." She fixed her own bowl. "Just a little surprised by your name."

"Why is that?" Don asked.

"I don't know. Expected something more exotic."

My fork dropped from my hand and clanked against the bowl when I realized why she was poking around about his name.

"More exotic? Why?" he asked.

"Because you're—"

"From Canada," I interrupted. "You're from Canada. Maybe she expected something French."

"Oh, he's not French," Helen said. "I know the French. French men have this thing about their nose."

Don laughed. "Their noses? And no, I wouldn't say I am French."

I cleared my throat. "You said you're from Saskatchewan. Do you still live there or do you live in America now?"

"No, I still live there."

"You're a long ways from home," Helen said. "Were you evacuating?"

"No, I haven't been home since the weather phenomenon started. I had been traveling, doing a series of lectures at the universities on the Cree Mythology, history and culture."

"Are you Cree?" I asked.

He nodded. "I am. And this"—he looked at Helen—"is very good."

"Thank you," Helen replied. "Are you a professor, writer, or just a lecturer?"

"I'm a professor," he replied. "I teach history. What about you?"

"Oh, I'm a retired crossing guard. Mac here worked for the local magistrate. That's a low-level judge." She winked. "So we're both in a weird way in law enforcement." She laughed at her own joke.

I shook my head and sipped my brandy. "Do you have family, Don?"

"Yes. I have a large family. Brothers and sisters, my parents. I was married once, we're divorced, no children."

"Did your family evacuate?" I asked.

"I hope so. I've not been able to get in touch with them."

"Speaking of evacuation," Helen said. "Everyone had a designated time and place. What happens with you?"

"Oh, I was given an evacuation pass and left when New York began to evacuate."

"That's a good thing," I said. "You have papers to get on the highway."

"I do. They just didn't give me a definite place to go," he said. "They gave me a list I can use to try to get into one of the relocation camps."

"Nonsense." Helen flung out her hand. "You'll stay at my brother Fred's house. That's where we're going. He's twelve miles out from the relocation camp. You'll stay with us. His house is big enough."

"That's very kind. But I can't ask that of you."

"You're not asking. We're telling. You saved our lives. You're taking us south. You…you are taking us, south, right?" she asked.

"I will take you both as far as we can go," he said.

"What does that mean?" I asked.

"It means we don't know what the weather holds. We may have to walk or find a different transportation," Don answered.

"But you said the weather isn't bad," I said.

"It isn't to me...yet. We have to assume something bigger is coming. There is a reason they are moving everyone south. We'll keep traveling south. And just hope we get there before the weather changes those plans."

"Do you think it will?" I asked.

"I don't know. I know as much as you." He shrugged. "Only time and days will tell."

TWELVE

STALL

August 3

The snap and crackle of the fire caused me to wake. I had fallen asleep hard. The events of the day before, along with the brandy, had knocked me out. I listened to the storm brewing outside, the thunder and pelting rain. It was my white noise, causing me to fall asleep earlier than Helen or Don.

Before I even opened my eyes, I thought of my family. I had an overwhelming feeling of dread that I tried to dismiss.

It was being away from them, the not knowing that had me fearful. My husband, son and daughter. Were they okay? Alive? Warm? Did they make it south, or did they, like us, have to stop?

When I finally gathered the strength to face the morning, I opened my eyes.

It was light outside.

There was something about the brightness of the day that was strange. It had a Christmas morning feel to it. Maybe it was the cold in the air. Though it was warm by the fire, I could tell the house was chilled.

I could smell the coffee. I sat up bringing the blanket over my shoulders. Helen was asleep in the chair. I saw two empty cups by the fireplace, near where I slept.

The old tin percolator was on the edge near the fire to keep warm. I figured Don must have made it and put two cups there for a reason, and I reached for the handle of the pot.

There was a rag tied to it—the handle was probably hot—and I poured some in a cup.

When I sat back to take a sip, I saw Don standing by the window, coffee cup in hand, intermittently drinking it while looking.

"Morning," I said.

"Morning," he replied.

"Boy, these people had everything. Even a camping coffee pot."

"That's mine. I grabbed it from a thrift store a week ago."

"Well, thank you for the coffee. I didn't even hear you get up."

"You were out cold. Recovering."

"Everything okay?" I asked.

He waved his hand for me to come over.

I stood with my coffee and walked toward that window.

"We need to leave soon," he said.

"What's going on?"

He pointed and his index finger pressed against the glass. I stepped in front of the window to see and realized at that second why it had that Christmas morning feeling.

I truly wasn't ready for what I saw.

It was a whole new ball game. After nearly a month, I was used to looking out the window to the gray skies so dark it could have been nightfall. I was used to the rain steadily falling, whether thick, snow filled or pure water. I wasn't ready at all to see snow.

The sky seemed brighter; it wasn't really. A pure optical illusion brought on by the reflecting snow. It didn't fall heavily, but at a steady rate. It barely looked as if it was enough to accumulate, yet it did. A fresh layer blanketed everything, except for the truck. It was evident Don had cleared that.

"Wow, when did this start?" I asked.

"A few hours ago. On a positive note it is four degrees warmer than yesterday," Don replied.

"Heatwave," I said sarcastically.

"It will feel much warmer. It was pretty cold yesterday and wet."

"This is wet."

"A different wet."

I brough the coffee to my lips and shivered. "It looks bad."

"It's not bad."

"Are you sure?" I asked.

He glanced at me.

"That's right. Canada."

"No, you shouldn't think it's bad either. It's only about three inches. Not bad at all. And I'll let you know when I think it's bad."

"So you've said."

He pressed his lips together in a closed-mouth smile.

I glanced over my shoulder to Helen. "I suppose we should wake her."

"We should. Let her have her coffee. Let's get something in our stomachs and we'll head out within the hour. We need to use as much daylight as possible. We have a lot to cover today."

"What do you mean?" I asked.

"Not only are we traveling south, we're looking for your family. They may have stopped, been sent to a camp or are waiting to go, or they could be stranded. I mean the truck did go in the river. Unless you want to just go straight south."

"No. No. Thank you. We'll look for them."

He gave me a nod, then turned back to the window, bringing the coffee to his lips. I walked away with a plan to finish my own beverage by the remaining fire then I would wake Helen.

She wasn't the least bit surprised when she saw the snow. She barely blinked, projecting an, *Oh, yes, there it is*. I was expecting that attitude. Merely glancing out the window then placing items she found in the house into a bag. I asked her what she was taking and she responded, "Things in case we have to walk. You'll thank me."

I was sure I would.

I didn't want to dismiss anything that Helen was doing. Her little tricks I often would make fun of were actually useful and resourceful. Her little extra bag was stuffed, but it didn't seem heavy. She carried it herself and toted it with ease when we left the house.

It was dumb, I knew, but I left a note on the kitchen table thanking the owners. I also made sure we didn't leave it a mess. I would hope the same would happen back home if a stranger found themselves having to stay in my house.

Just before eight in the morning, later than Don wanted to go, we made our way to the truck. The snow was already another half an inch deeper than when I first saw it and a thin layer had formed on the truck.

He didn't start the car early to let it warm up. That told me even without him saying he was worried about gas.

Our gas canister was in the back of the truck and I knew he hadn't touched it yet, so that was a good thing.

Even though I was an experienced driver in the snow, I was glad Don from Canada was driving. Not only was driving going to take skill, it would take instincts and memory, because there were no tire tracks, no plow marks, just a virgin coat of snow on the road covering everything in a smooth way, masking even the curves and bends.

"This looks bad," I said.

"Nah, it's fine," Don replied as he drove.

"What happened to the water?" I asked. "The slush?"

"Frozen beneath us."

He said it nonchalantly. I knew there was no controlling a slide on ice. Even the best cars or trucks with the greatest tires. Nothing made a difference on ice. The snow at least was giving us traction. I didn't feel us sliding at all if we were.

"Aren't you afraid you'll go off the road?" I asked.

"No, because there isn't anything I can do about it. We'll know, we'll feel it. I'm taking it slow. I made two trips down this road. I don't remember any surprises."

He seemed confident and focused on his driving. I stayed quiet because I didn't want to distract him. He had told us it was only about five miles to the highway. He believed it would be different there. People were still evacuating from further north.

I hoped he was right.

I had to remind myself just because we didn't see tire tracks didn't mean anything. More than likely everyone on the south side of the river in Pennsburg had probably left, and since the bridge was down no one was traveling that road.

About twenty minutes into our slow-moving journey, I felt the truck slow down and then stop.

"What's wrong?" I asked.

Don pointed ahead.

Not far away I could see movement. Not fast movement, but vehicles none the less.

I exhaled. "Is that the highway?"

"It's the highway," Don replied. "The ramp is just a little ways up. It's a low-grade entrance ramp, but even if it's snow covered we shouldn't have any trouble. The cars are moving, so the snow is not holding things back."

That was a good thing

However, I had to wonder what world I lived in. A part of me was stuck in the normal mentality that when road crews didn't do the side streets, at least the main roads would be clear. In my mind we'd zip up that ramp and emerge to a wet highway.

I was wrong on the zip.

Don kept the pressure on the pedal steady but there was so much ice, I worried we'd burned through a ton of gasoline.

We spun and slid on the low-grade ramp, then finally we lunged forth onto the highway and spun again.

He apologized, but it wasn't his fault.

There were tire tracks, no plow marks, and all the cars did was push down the snow making the roads even more treacherous. It wasn't the usual snowy highway driving, where some jerk saw you driving slow and thought they had a better vehicle or better control and passed you like a maniac. Everyone moved the same speed.

With caution.

Not even twenty miles into our trip, we started to see flares set up on the snowy banks of the highway. One every hundred feet on both sides of the road.

They not only reflected against the snow, they even melted it a little.

"What's this?" Don asked, leaning into the wheel.

"A detour?" Helen guessed.

I glanced to Helen then down to her lap. She clutched a small, burgundy bag on her lap. She'd found it at the house and had put in items from there as well. I had to wonder what she had that she was holding onto so protectively.

I wasn't even going to venture a guess out loud as to what the flares were for. It didn't matter. Not long after seeing them they led toward the side of the road and soon enough a military truck came into view.

"Is this one of those checkpoints? I asked. "Where they check your pass?"

"No, it's not. At least it isn't like the other day," Don replied.

We watched as the line of cars slowly came together to form a tight-knit traffic jam. One female soldier waved them on. Some cars stopped, she'd lean in, speak to them and then they'd drive through.

Some cars didn't stop. I didn't get that. Weren't they curious or was it something they were used to seeing?

It took us ten minutes to reach the soldier and Don stopped, rolling down his window. The blowing snow came in the window and I felt bad for the young solider. She had to be cold as the snow built up on the shoulders of her jacket and her hat.

"I know you've gotten this question a lot," Don said. "Something happen?"

"We're moving all cars off the highway, sir. Please move forward." She stepped back.

"Okay," Don sung out the word, tapped his hand on the steering wheel and then leaned back out again. "That's not an acceptable answer. Can I ask why?"

"Move forward please, follow the line of traffic," was her response, never batting an eye or getting annoyed. She just waved her arm like she had probably done a thousand times already for the day.

There were no answers, not from her anyway. Maybe there would be down the road.

But the flare-lit roadway led off a down decent-size exit ramp which was packed with cars all waiting to go somewhere.

The only positive thing about the traffic on the ramp was the underbellies of the cars and trucks melted the snow and ice enough that we weren't sliding. Then again, we had to be moving to slide.

"Are you angry?" I asked Don. "I can't tell."

"I'm not angry. I'm not happy, she could have said the road was closed, stated the reason and then waved her arm."

"Would it have mattered?" I asked.

"What do you mean?" Don asked. "Of course it would have mattered. She would have told us something."

"But…I mean, you would have had another question. I'm sure. Like maybe for how long. Where are we going, that sort of thing. I think this is best. Whenever we really stop up ahead then we can have our answers. Nothing we can do about it."

Helen huffed at me. "Why are you trying to poke a bear?"

"I'm not poking any bear, I'm trying to ease his mind."

"The man doesn't look like his mind needs eased," Helen argued. "You just have to pick a fight with everyone."

"Ladies," Don spoke softly.

"What do you mean, I pick a fight with everyone."

"I'm sorry," Helen said. "Men, you pick fights with men. You always have."

"Are you talking about your son?" I asked.

"Ladies."

"Because," I said, "husbands don't count."

"Husbands count," Helen said. "You're always picking a fight with him. And your boss. How many times do you come home and tell us you fought with your boss?"

"He's my boss," I defended.

"Ladies."

"Keep going," I said. "Name another time."

"Getting groceries."

When she said that, my blood immediately boiled. "Oh my God, you didn't."

"What?" she asked.

"Oh my God."

"Ladies."

"I can't believe you."

"What?" Helen asked.

"Grocery store."

"Yes. You want to deny it?"

"I won't deny it, I just can't believe you brought that up. You're so freaking heartless," I blasted. "What? You want to say I am also a cold-blooded murderer, huh? Say I picked a fight with that man and killed him on purpose?"

The cab of the truck grew instantly quiet.

"Um." Helen cleared her throat. "No. I wasn't. I was talking about Marv at Stockey's."

"Oh, shit, yeah." I cringed. "I did fight with him." I peered over her to Don, who stared straight ahead. "Don, listen…"

"Nope." He shook his head. "Don't care. Don't want to know. Just stop…fighting, please."

We did.

The off-ramp journey reminded me of waiting to go into the parking for an outdoor rock concert. Only the parking guy was replaced with a soldier that waved us into the lot of a super center located a half mile from the exit. They directed people to park in what seemed like an orderly fashion, then we'd all pull back out and head to the highway when the time came.

Seemed fair enough.

We were fairly close to the lot exit so we'd get there easily. I could even see the highway.

Once we realized we were going to be there for a little bit, Don shut off the engine. It didn't take long after the wipers went down for a layer of snow to form on the windshield.

It was that fast.

"I'll be back. Keep the doors locked." Don reached for his door handle.

"Where are you going?" I asked.

"I'm going to find out what's going on."

Immediately, I grabbed for my door handle. "I'll go with you."

"That's alright. You should stay here where it's warm," he suggested.

"No, I'd like to go. Is that okay, Helen? Will you be okay?" I asked.

"Oh, sure, I'll lock the doors. I'll be fine." She patted her bag. "And don't forget your hat and gloves."

She was right. I was ready to get out of the truck without them. I saw Don was waiting for me before he opened the door so I hurried in getting ready. Before putting on my gloves, I pulled the plastic bonnet out of my coat pocket and secured it tightly on my head with the visor portion closer to my eyebrows, then I put the knit cap over that, put on my gloves and opened the door.

The wind was pretty strong, blowing the snow in multiple directions.

I pushed the door closed and in a role reversal I pointed to the door for Helen to lock it. When she did, I pulled my hood up and walked to the front of the truck to meet up with Don.

"What's the plan?" I asked.

"Find one of the soldiers." He gave a twitch of his head as his way of pointing.

The snow was heavy and deep in areas cars had not driven over. "Now, will you admit it's bad?" I asked.

"Not yet."

I wanted to call bullshit on that, he was just humoring me. I stayed close to him, even though it was hard to keep up with his stride. He seemed to have an easier time moving in the snow than I did.

Cars were still pulling down the ramp, and traffic backed up to the highway. But the bright spot was there was a last car.

Two male soldiers were there, one stood at the entrance of the parking lot, the other in the street directed traffic. There was a third but he was way in the back. We aimed for the two on the street.

Don walked toward the first young soldier, almost as if he had a plan. The soldier didn't look much older than my son. He wore a parka, but a lot of good it did. He had it opened and when we approached I could see the name 'Flint' on the tag above his pocket on the cover jacket he wore underneath.

The mother in me wanted to tell Flint to close his coat.

"Excuse me, son," Don called the young man. "Any chance you can tell us what's going on?"

"Sure. We're clearing the highway. Government is sending a plow. Got a storm coming."

"This isn't it?" I asked

He smiled and shook his head. "No, ma'am, it isn't. They want to clear this before it gets really bad."

"If you ask him," I said with a point to Don, "this isn't bad."

Flint chuckled. "I hear it isn't compared to what is coming. So that's what's going on. Once the plow comes by we will let everyone head out."

"Do you know when that will be?" Don asked.

"Not sure. Soon, now that all the cars are off the highway. Shouldn't take long. They did the same thing yesterday to get the ice and slush off."

"They cleared the road yesterday?" Don asked. "How far south?"

"At least to west Virginia. Not all at the same time," Flint said.

"Of course," Don replied. "Were you here yesterday?"

"Me? No."

"Do you know what time they did this yesterday?" Don questioned further.

"Afternoon. Early. Not morning, I know that. Right before they shut the road down."

"I dropped some people off at a military truck yesterday, the bridge collapsed."

"Ah, yeah." He nodded. "I heard about that."

"Do you know what happened to those people?"

"I'm sorry, I don't. I wasn't here," Flint said.

"Is there anyone here that was here yesterday?" Don asked.

Flint shook his head. "We all go south in groups. We left Binghamton this morning. They closed this highway at four yesterday. So those folks you brought here stopped for the night down on 95. If not farther. Sorry I couldn't be more help."

"No, you've been a great help," Don said. "How long will this take?"

"Soon as the plows pull through, we'll start pulling you guys out. That's what I was told. Wanna get you on the road before it gets bad. Wait. Whoops." He pointed. "You don't think it's bad."

Don smiled and thanked him again.

Then I thanked him and of course couldn't resist telling him, "Zip up your coat."

We took a few steps away and Don stopped. "Zip up your coat?"

"I've been wanting to say that since we approached him."

"That's funny. So, basically, we're here for a couple hours tops. Hit the road again. And they'll probably make us pull over somewhere on 95."

"That's what it sounds like," I said.

"Figuring your family got a ride, they probably are south of Philly right now. They're a day ahead, maybe not even. They have to stop at night when we do."

"Which is a good thing," I told him.

"It is. We're on the same route. Heck, they probably stopped in this same lot." He crinkled his brow with curiosity, looking at me.

"What?"

He reached up and swiped my visor clearing the snow. "It's really coming down. You have a good half inch on that contraption you're wearing."

"Don't make fun of this thing. It's the warmest my head has ever felt."

"Not making fun."

"You know Helen has a couple. She'll give you one," I joked.

"I may have to ask…" He paused and shifted his eyes.

"What's wrong?" I asked. "More snow somewhere else?" Even though at that moment I tried to joke, I saw the sudden seriousness and concern on his face. "Don?"

Focused, he brushed by me, merely mumbling, "Come on."

He didn't walk in the direction of the truck.

"Where are we going?"

"Something I see. I need to check."

"What do you see?"

"Just follow me. And hope I'm wrong."

"I hope you're wrong," I said, walking with him. I had no idea what he was talking about or what he believed he saw. Whatever it was worried him.

Not only did we not move in the direction of the truck, we totally walked away from the lot, staying on the street. He moved fast, faster than I could keep up with and when we reached the end of the super center parking lot, the road disappeared beneath the snow.

No footprints or tire marks, nothing.

I wanted to ask him again where we were going, but Don knew. He knew what he saw and we'd eventually confirm or deny whatever it was.

Someone hollered at us, saying we were going the wrong way. That nothing was down there.

Probably Flint.

What did Don see?

After walking a good solid, city-size block after the super center parking lot, Don stopped.

I caught up and noticed we were at the entrance of another parking lot, a Home Depot one.

I had to catch my breath.

"Is this what you saw?" I asked.

"A Home Depot," he said.

"Yes, it is."

"During a major exodus. So why is the lot full?"

I gasped out a whispering, "Oh my God," when I finally saw through the optical illusion of the white, blanketed lot.

It was full, hundreds upon hundreds of vehicles. The cars and lot were covered and camouflaged with untouched snow.

Like cars left for the winter in a used car lot, only it was a Home Depot.

Scarier than the sight of all those cars, was the fact that they were all parked the exact same way we were at the super center.

Don moved with urgency, tromping through the snow.

I hesitated to follow at first, then I did.

He didn't go far into the lot, just to the first car. He held his hand to the driver's side window and looked over his shoulder at me.

I nodded and watched him take a deep breath, just before he cleared the snow on the window.

Under the snow, the window was iced over with a thin layer giving it a rippled appearance, but still clear enough for me to see there was a man inside. His head was arched back, mouth and eyes open, his skin pale blue.

We didn't need to open the car door to know the man was dead.

Dead behind the wheel of his car, parked in a lot in an orderly fashion, probably waiting…just like us.

THIRTEEN

GLASS HALF FULL

My immediate reaction was to believe the man in the car was a fluke. Not taking into consideration there were so many cars.

"Jesus, Don," I said, looking at the man. "How long would he have had to be out here to die from the cold?"

"Eight to ten hours," Don replied. "I think they moved them from the highway to plow and the cars couldn't get back on."

In the midst of truly comprehending what he said it finally hit me. I spun left to right, looking around. This wave of crushing fear, crippling panic overtook me. I couldn't move, I couldn't think of anything other than my children, my husband, how they probably pulled off the road right there. "My family could be here. My family could be in one of these cars."

Instantly he kicked into gear. Staying calm, he walked to the next car in line and swiped his hand over the windshield. "No kids." He went to the next one. "None." The next. "Empty." On the fourth car, after swiping, he stopped. He didn't announce what he saw, he just stepped to the side to allow me to look.

That first car was the hardest. My heart pounded so fast I could barely breathe. Then I peeked into the small space. It wasn't them. They were blurry from the iced windows, but clear enough for me to see. A family: the children were small, they had blankets over them, one even had a juice box.

It truly made me sad.

I shook my head and Don walked to the next one. There was no doubt in my mind that he would swipe the snow from every car, no matter how long it took, to know and see if my family was there.

The first row was the hardest, and it was easy when we hit the second row. Midway through that, we worked more together to do things faster.

We both removed snow from cars. If he saw children, he called for me.

Fortunately, over half were empty.

Increasingly, I grew worried, fearful of that old saying *it's always the last place you look*. Eight rows of cars and we weren't halfway through, but we were moving pretty quickly.

I didn't notice the cold or snow, I was determined.

Midway through the fourth row, another soldier approached us. We were so focused we didn't see him coming. He was more winter ready than Flint. Knit cap, zippered, dark googles, and a scarf that was pulled to just below his bottom lip.

"Is there something you're looking for, folks?" he asked. "My men said you're over here in the cars."

Don immediately stopped, his attention drawn to this man, and he made his way over to him.

"Your men?" Don asked. "Are you in charge?"

"I am. I'm Captain Holland."

"Captain, are you aware," Don said firmly, "that there are bodies in these cars? A lot of bodies. It looks to me that they were waiting on something."

I watched the captain. Having worked for years at the magistrate, I was pretty good at judging the facial reactions of people. His bottom lip moved as he tensed it.

"No," he said calmly. "Will you excuse me." He took a step away, then stopped. "Are you looking for something in particular or just seeing how many bodies there are?"

"I'm looking for my family," I replied. "My husband and children. We got separated when the bridge washed out. They may have gotten a ride."

He nodded, nothing more, and then he walked away.

I didn't know what that was about, but Don and I returned to checking the cars. Not even five minutes later, four soldiers came over.

"What do they look like, what are we looking for?" one of them asked.

I told them to look for a teenage boy and a five-year-old girl. If I would have described Glen, that would have fit the description of half the men I knew. I could have run back to the truck and got my phone, showed a picture, but that wasn't necessary.

The captain sent them to help. Each of them seemed genuinely surprised that the lot was a cemetery.

They did the same as us, cleared snow, peeked in and looked. I was grateful. With the additional help we were able to finish the search.

My family, my children weren't there.

I hoped and prayed they were safely with the others that weren't in the cars. Every couple of minutes, I'd reach into my big pockets and grasp onto Cleo's shoe.

We had been so busy I didn't notice if the plows had come. It had taken us a little under an hour with the help to search all the cars.

Once I realized the length of time, I worried about Helen. Did she start the truck for heat, fall asleep, and die of hypothermia?

On the walk back to our own lot, we picked up the pace and the captain found us.

"Got a minute?" he asked.

"Considering we aren't allowed to move," Don replied. "We have the time." He spoke in a mild-mannered way, being pretty facetious.

"I radioed HQ," Holland said. "They had no idea the motorists had died. What they told me was they had cars pull off the road, like this. They plowed the ice. This lot was actually used yesterday as well. The ice and rain kept coming, motorists ran out of gas, they had two evac buses pick up people. Some opted to stay and wait out the weather, some walked, others braved the road, and some waited for a gas truck that...never came."

Don lifted his head to the falling snow. "If that plow doesn't come soon, it will happen again."

"I agree. I'm on it. I will make sure every car gets out or at least every person. There are two buses arriving. Some cars are already out of gas."

"What about a gas truck?" Don asked.

"They come from the south. One won't come up. We're going to ask people to take others. I am confident we can get everyone out. We don't have nearly the people they had yesterday from what I have been told."

"Do you believe what you were told?" Don asked.

"I do."

"You realize if you would have let traffic keep flowing, they would have cleared the roads enough."

"In a sense," Holland said. "You also have people that would run out of gas and accidents. Then the plows can't get through at all."

"Are they even coming?" Don asked.

"We hope."

"Thank you." Don turned and walked away. I followed next to him.

I kept thinking about those people that died in their cars, and the ones that walked away. Did they regret not getting on the evacuation bus or asking someone for a ride? Maybe there just wasn't a choice and they stayed behind knowing they would die.

It was an incredibly sad fate they faced.

"What do you think?" I asked.

"I think if that plow doesn't come in an hour, we're leaving. This is falling an inch an hour, we can still travel the roads. We may have to stop again for the night though."

"But when we get south we should run into less snow."

"One would think," Don replied. "But we still have a long ways to go until we get out of the snow belt area."

I paused in my walking when I saw the truck. The windows were completely covered with snow. I rushed over really concerned for Helen.

When I arrived I threw open the passenger door, causing Helen to jump and grab her chest.

"You scared me," she said.

"Sorry," I said. "Are you alright?"

"I am."

"I thought you froze to death."

Helen chuckled. "Hardly, I'm good. Warm."

"How?" I asked, then saw the cord that came from under her coat into the cigarette lighter. "What is this?"

"Heating pad for the car. I found it in that house. You want to use it?"

"Yes, please. Thank you."

Helen pulled it from her coat and handed it to me. It took getting into the car for me to realize how cold I truly was. Immediately, I shoved it in my own coat and absorbed the instant warmth. I couldn't believe she held out on us. I'd share it with Don as soon as I felt a little warmer.

"Did you get any information?" Helen question.

"Some," Don replied as he got in the truck. "Plow should be here, there are going to be a couple evacuation buses as well."

"Let's hope they don't leave us here," Helen said.

Both Don and I immediately looked forward.

"What? What did I say?" she asked.

"Don saw another parking lot. It had a lot of cars in it. They were covered with snow," I said. "There were cars pulled over yesterday and the cars were full of dead bodies."

"Yesterday?" Helen questioned. "Did you look to see if Glen…"

A nod of my head stopped her mid-sentence.

"Not there?" she asked.

I shook my head. "We looked."

Helen sighed out. "So that's what you were doing. I saw you walking the other way."

"Weren't you curious where we were going?" I asked.

"No," Helen replied. "I saw the Home Depot sign and figured you two were going to find a kerosene heater. I thought, wow, that's smart. A portable heating source. Because it's August and the heaters and kerosene would be in the back in seasonal. No one had time to bring it from the back before everything shut down. But…I guess not."

Don opened his door.

"Where are you going now?" I asked.

"Where do you think?" He stepped out. "Gonna look for that kerosene heater."

The huge billows of snow that blew upward and spiraled were a beautiful sight to see when the snowplows made their way down the highway.

Don had been gone a half an hour when they arrived; I was sorry he missed it.

Not by much, though. He returned with a box and his fingers clenching the handle of a plastic gallon container. He took it to the back, lifted the tarp, and placed it in before getting back inside.

"Did you get a good one?" I asked.

"I got one that will work for us. I was thinking if we get stuck outside," he replied. "Let's hope that doesn't happen. As long as we find some sort of shelter we can be warm."

I leaned toward the windshield I had cleared not five minutes before and it was covered again. "He said there's a storm coming. It's coming down pretty good now. I wonder what this storm means?"

"I'll tell you what it means," Helen said. "If they're saying a storm is coming that means, somewhere out there, somebody is predicting the weather, and that means, this country hasn't shut down completely. Not yet."

Helen had a point. Who was predicting the weather? The captain had radioed 'headquarters' but what did that mean and where was that? We may have been in desolation, but other parts of the world weren't. That was encouraging.

It was also encouraging to see cars leaving the parking lot just as the two dark green buses pulled up.

Yet, we weren't moving. Don hadn't turned on the ignition.

"We aren't leaving, too?" I asked.

"We are," Don replied. "We're waiting."

"For?" I asked.

He pointed at the buses. "Them. We'll follow them as far as they go. They have chains on the wheels and look at the front ends. Small plows attached. They will clear the way."

"That's good thinking, Don," Helen said.

The triple tap on Don's window took us all by surprise. We couldn't see who it was, just a figure. Don rolled down the window and the snow blew into the truck until Flint leaned in and blocked it.

"Hey, I know you folks said you're looking for family," he said. "Plan is to stop the buses just before Wilmington before the storm. There's a rest camp there with a fuel truck. That's where the plow came from. Just thought you may want to stop there as well. It's been a stopping point for the last two weeks. Same people volunteer there. If you have a picture, you may want to ask around. Someone may have seen them, especially since they would have been there yesterday."

I believed a smile crossed my face, not only for the information, but because the young man took the time to come over and tell us that, to acknowledge my quest was more than just heading south.

"Thank you. Thank you so very much," I told him. "I appreciate that."

"Be safe," he said. "And look...I zipped up." Flint flashed a smile, then walked away.

While sitting there waiting to pull out and follow the bus, I had a glimmer of hope. One that was needed, especially after looking in all those cars. There was a chance, albeit small, someone at the next stop would have seen my family. Perhaps someone there could tell me they were alright.

More than anything, I needed to hear they were.

FOURTEEN

SIDE CAMP

I didn't believe for one second when Don said it wasn't bad. Was he nuts or did he just live shy of the north pole? The snow fell steadily and we moved at a snail's pace, which wasn't an exaggeration. The buses moved no more than twenty-five miles per hour top speed, and what made matters worse were the cars who tried to pass them. Every five miles or so we'd slow down to a halt while the soldiers helped the drivers out of the snow or onto the bus.

For a brief moment, the sky was bright and the snow stopped. *What was all the talk about a storm?*

Then the clouds rolled in. As fast as they parted they threw us into an unusual darkness, blowing the snow from the roads like a cyclone.

That storm they'd warned about was coming.

We pulled into the camp just outside of Wilmington. I truly didn't understand them positioning it so close to the water. Not that I could see it, but I knew where we were and knew it was colder and windier near any lake, river, or ocean.

The camp, though, was shielded in a weird way. It was expediently erected on a construction site. A huge privacy tarp fence surrounded the water side, blocking a lot of the wind.

The ground-level framing was put to use; tents had been attached to the metal framing to create walls. Round tubing ran up to the ceiling as ventilation for the woodburning stoves. That was the main portion. A canteen, a medical area and cots had been set up.

Other tents were erected as well as a few small trailers that belonged to those who worked there daily. It was a transient stop. A place for those relocating to pause for the night, have a meal and get some fuel.

Next to the construction site was another super center and we were directed to park there.

After getting a good parking spot a stone's throw from the camp, we brought our belongings with us, leaving nothing in the truck. It was the first time I really saw what Don had.

He secured one of those huge hiker packs on his back. It had a sleeping roll and probably everything else he needed.

Even in the short distance, the wind was unbelievably cold and my nose felt numb after only a few minutes outside.

There was no order, no registration, and I wondered without any of that, would getting information on my family even be possible?

Captain Holland was kind enough to explain how it worked. The soldiers got the exterior tents and unless we wanted to stay in the truck, we just had to find space inside. It was first come, first served.

The main makeshift tent was bigger than a gymnasium. It was divided: to the left was the canteen, center was a small section with nurses and to the right was where everyone settled for the night.

We found a spot before anything else. A nice corner toward the front. It wasn't too cold in the tent at all. Don said if need be he'd fire up the kerosene heater.

We set our belongings around us like a fort for privacy, but that wasn't necessary. No one really was in the mood to talk to anyone else.

Helen saw it differently. She wanted her privacy and to be left alone. She sat on the cot, blanket around her shoulders while she sipped out of that bottle of brandy she'd found at the house.

Don dropped his gear, lay down his sleeping roll and disappeared. It was still early and there was a lot of motion in the tent and I could smell something really good. It hit me that I hadn't really eaten anything all day.

"You think the food is free?" I asked Helen.

"Oh, I don't know. Did you bring money?" she asked.

"Not cash."

"I don't think they accept debit. Hold on." She grabbed her backpack and reached into the front pocket pulling out a five-dollar bill. "Here. Just in case."

"Thank you. Did you want anything?"

"If you can get me, you and Don something on that five, then great. If not, you first, then Don. I have this"—she pointed to the bottle—"and some saltines. I'm good."

"Better slow down on that." I pointed to the brandy. "You don't know when you'll find another bottle."

"Sure I do. When I'm done with this, there's another in my pack."

That made me smile, and with that five-dollar bill clenched in my hand, I walked across the large tented area to where they were serving food.

There were two women and a man. The man was off to the side, looking as if he was watching for trouble while the women worked the food line.

There was one person in line, and I watched the woman behind the large cauldron serve him something in a large cup.

I approached her. "Smells wonderful."

"Potato soup. Not much but it will fill your belly."

"How much?"

"Oh, no honey, it's free," she said sweetly.

"I'll have some. And could I get a helping for my mother-in-law?"

"Absolutely."

"Thank you."

"Hey," Don called out as he approached and stood next to me.

"Hey. Where were you?"

"Making sure…no matter what we are moving forward tomorrow."

"Is there a reason we wouldn't be?" I asked.

"Weather. Not that it's bad…"

"No. Not at all."

"But I was making sure we could."

"And can we?"

"Yep. We're good."

The woman serving food asked Don if he wanted any and he accepted with politeness.

We took our large paper cups of soup, a roll and bottle of water back to our corner where Helen had a big three-wick candle lit.

"What the hell?" I asked, handing her the soup. "What all do you have in that bag?"

"Enough. You'll thank me."

"And this isn't sarcastic," I said as I sat on the ground, "I'm sure I will. If I haven't already, thank you."

"Plastic bonnet?"

"I love it."

117

"I knew it…" She lifted her spoon, pointing it at me before she got stuck into her soup. "I swear by them. Always have. Used them every day as a crossing guard. Even in the worst snowstorms and that was back in the day when they didn't cancel school over two inches of snow."

"Wait," Don said. "You cancel school over a few inches of snow?"

"Yeah," I answered. "Don't you?'

Don laughed. "No. We have to have at least six inches before they even call a delay."

"Wow, no wonder this weather isn't bad to you." I finally tried my soup. It was hearty and warm and tasted good.

"Did you ask the food person?" Helen quizzed.

"I'm sorry, ask the food person…what?" I asked.

"If they saw the kids, Glen? I mean, they gave food, they may have if they were feeding people yesterday."

"No, I didn't." I set down my cup. "That's a great idea. I will now." I reached for my backpack, being careful not to cause our little fort to tumble and I pulled out my phone. Quickly I went to the photos to find one with Glen and the kids. I found one of Glen and Cleo which would do, then I stood.

"Did you need me to come with you?" Don asked.

"No, I'm good, stay with Helen."

After telling them I'd be back, I stood and hurried back over to the food line.

"That was fast," the woman pleasantly said. "Ready for another."

"No. I'm…I'm not back for food. Were you serving the food in the line yesterday?"

"I work with the food every day. For the most part I was handing it out," she replied.

"I got separated from my family." I lifted my phone. "Can you look and see if you saw them?"

She took the phone and studied the picture. "No, I'm sorry. Can't say that I have. That doesn't mean they weren't here."

"I know." I took the phone.

"How did you get separated?" she asked.

"Up in Pennsburg. The bridge washed away. Me and my mother-in-law were on it."

"Wait a second…maybe." She looked to her left and called out, "Hey, Suze, didn't someone mention yesterday about that bridge in Pennsburg washing out. People that lost family."

"Yeah, someone was talking about it," Suze replied. "I remember that. They lost their family. I remember thinking how horrible."

I gasped a little and with my phone hurried to her. "Maybe you saw them."

Suze took the phone. "He looks familiar." She pointed to Glen.

"Bob Abbot," a male voice called out. "It was Bob Abbot."

I turned to the voice. It was the man who was standing off to the side.

"Are you sure, Merle?" Suze asked.

"Yep. Bob's good people." He looked at me. "I've known Bob for years. He's a truck driver by trade. In fact, he was headed north looking for his own family and ended up picking up a bunch of people from that downed bridge. He has that deluxe range rover thingy. Whatever."

"Did you see any of those people?" I asked. "Any of the ones he grabbed?"

"One or two," Merle answered.

"Maybe you can look. Me and my mother-in-law were in our truck when the bridge washed away." I walked to him holding out the phone with the picture showing. "My husband and kids"

"Yep." Merle nodded. "Saw him. In fact, Bob told us he watched his wife and mother wash down river."

I peeped a shriek of delight. "Oh my God, thank you." I hugged him. "What about the girl? Did you see the girl?"

"I can't say that I did," Merle replied.

Suze interjected. "But I know Bob had kids in that vehicle of his."

"He did," Merle said. "He was taking the I95 corridor all the way to Georgia. Some relocation camp. I know this because he's hoping to find his own family there."

"Do you know where? I mean, I don't expect you to. But…"

"Barry…Raintree …"

"Bainbridge?"

Merle snapped his finger. "That's it."

"Oh!" I hugged him again. "Thank you. Thank you so much. I have to tell my mother-in-law. Thank you."

I rambled my gratitude and, suddenly feeling renewed, I hurried back toward the sleeping portion of the tent. I was filled with some sort of optimistic energy.

It had only been a day.

One day.

The second overnight place.

I had my answers.

What were the odds?

Stop.

Really…what were the odds?

I froze in my tracks overwhelmed with a feeling of panic and worry.

It was too easy.

Nothing ever came easy and I hoped the old saying *too good to be true* didn't hold up in my case.

<><><><>

Everyone slept.

The energy level of the tent grew as people settled, kids ran around, people talked, and then they all just tucked away early.

A hush of silence took over the tent.

The calm before the storm.

Then the predicted storm did come. Though, later than expected. It didn't seem to bother or wake anyone, no one stirred, no babies cried. Did anyone but me even hear it?

It was so bad I was afraid to look out.

The wind howled and the secured heavy tarp of the tents flapped violently. The cold seeped through and I found myself sitting close to Helen.

There was no way I could sleep, I didn't want to. My family was heavy on my mind.

I sat on the floor against Helen's cot, knees bent to my chest, one earphone in my ear watching videos of my kids on my phone while I held tight to the pink boot.

I was focused on the videos until I heard something 'whap' against the metal outside. It caused me to jump and then I noticed Don sit up.

"Did you hear that?" he asked.

"Yeah, the storm has arrived," I whispered.

"Did you look out?"

I shook my head.

He scooted his way over to sit by me, looking at what I was doing. "Are you alright?"

I shrugged.

"You seem down," he said.

"I am."

"Why?" he asked. "I mean, you should be happy. Merle saw your family."

"No," I said. "Merle saw my husband. He didn't see my children."

"Is that what you're thinking about?"

"I can't *not* think about it. I keep replaying my enthusiastically naive moment with him, not even registering that he said he only saw my husband."

"Just because he didn't see your children—"

"I know," I interrupted him. "And I keep telling myself that."

"And if someone came tomorrow and showed a picture of you and Helen to Merle, he could saw he only saw you."

"That's true."

"Mac, I'm not a father," Don said. "But I know if I was, there was no way I could go on if I lost everyone. At least keep traveling south. I couldn't do it. Could Glen?"

"I don't think he could. I couldn't."

"Exactly. Not this soon, he wouldn't move forward. The kids are with him. He had them protected and away from everyone. You need to believe it and you need that to move forward. We have a name of the man he's traveling with. We'll find them."

I exhaled heavily. "I hope you're right. I really do. Because I have been sitting here all night, watching videos, looking at pictures, embracing this"—I held up the shoe—"pink boot. Trying. Trying so hard to tap in. To find that psychic mother connection. When Aaron was nine he was in the scouts. His troop got lost in the woods. It was raining, the weather was horrible. I dug deep you know, and I knew, I felt it. He was fine. Everything was fine."

"This is a different situation. This is big with a lot of unknowns."

"And I am taking that into account. I'll keep going. I'll keep believing. I'll try my damndest to ignore the fact I'm trying as hard as I can to feel something. But, sadly," I said, "I don't feel them at all."

FIFTEEN

PINK SNOW

August 4

The line for the porta johns was almost as long as the line for the oatmeal. Both seemed ridiculous. I was glad I got up an hour or so before the rush and went back to sleep. We didn't need to get oatmeal, the granola we had in our packs would suffice.

I did, however, want to get a bottle of warm wash water and wash my face and arms.

The second time I woke up, Don was gone again. His things were still there and since I didn't spot him, I figured he was in the porta john line.

I waited for a little bit for one of the warm bottles that were in a hot water filled pan by the woodburning stove. I held it in my hands for a moment to warm them. I heard somebody say it was twenty degrees out with a negative windshield. I believed that. I was cold and followed the advice I was given to wear minimal layers inside for effectiveness of the layers outside.

There was a lot of chatter about the relocation camps that were being built, what they would be like. Someone said they thought it would be like the FEMA camps. After staying in the tent overnight,

I was starting to rethink the old prison refugee camps. At least there would be toilets.

After washing up, which didn't make me feel any better, I returned to our little corner to finish packing.

Things started buzzing. People were moving about, they were calling for bus riders like it was school, and there was oddly a lot of commotion. Not that I listened to what the commotion was about, I just wanted to leave.

Where was Don?

His hiker backpack was all ready to go, complete with the rope wrapped up again. He had used it the night before to string our belongings together in case someone decided to walk off with something while we slept.

Briefly, I worried that he was dead.

Then he showed up.

"You ladies ready, they're lining us up."

"Like prisoners?" I asked.

"No." He laughed. "Vehicles."

"Well, that's odd," Helen said. "Why would they do that?"

"The order of the vehicles has to do with road safety," Don said. "Some will clear the roads better than others."

"Where were you?" I questioned. "I know, I always seem to be asking that."

"That's fine. Making sure we were road ready. That we would have the least amount of problems traveling the roads."

Hating to ask, I said, "Is it bad?"

"It's getting there," he replied.

"Oh my God, a different answer. Will the truck be okay?" I asked.

"No." He shook his head. "I got us a new one. This will be much better. In fact, it has to get pretty bad for it not to keep going."

"Don," Helen said brightly. "You're so resourceful."

"Not really," he answered. "And this one comes with a price."

I wasn't sure what he meant by that. Did we have to give something up? I didn't ask because I was certain I'd find out soon enough.

Saddled up with all of our gear, we walked to the end of the tent and to the entrance where people were lined up to leave. I didn't understand the lining up. To me, we should just go when ready. Why were people waiting to leave?

Until I walked out.

My first reaction was to blast at Don, "Getting there?"

Did he seriously imply the weather was 'getting there' meaning it wasn't quite bad yet? To me, it was really bad.

I knew my initial reaction was spot on when Helen confirmed it by saying, "In all my years, I have never seen this much snow."

"I have," Don said.

"Well, we're not you," I rebutted. "This is insane."

"It's snow."

"No shit."

The reason everyone lined up at one exit was because it was the only exit that was cleared. The snow was three feet high and cars were buried in it. I felt bad for those cars having to dig out.

We walked down a cleared path and to a four-door, long cab pickup truck with a county emblem on the side and plow on the front.

"Is this it?" I asked.

"Yes, it is," Don answered.

"How did you get this?" I asked, impressed.

When Don placed our gear in the back, I could see the gas cans. "It wasn't as easy as it seems. Like I said there is a huge price to pay."

"This is impressive, Don," Helen told him as he held open the back door for her. He helped her, hoisting her up some to get into the back seat.

"Thank you."

I got inside and then Don did. He started the truck.

"Cozy," Helen commented. "Roomy too. I can stretch a bit. So nice. Do you think my heating pad cord will reach?" she asked.

"We can try."

"How did you pull this off? This is a big one," I said.

"I found someone in charge, then spoke to Captain Holland and told him that there is so much snow, the roads needed plowed constantly. Let the first plows clear part of the path, then smaller plows to pick up the drop off."

"That is brilliant," I told him. "I mean, that clears the way for all those in this camp that are headed south."

"It's safer," he said. "And I told him I was a plow driver for years."

"You never mentioned that. I didn't know."

"That's because I'm not," Don said. "I lied to get this. How hard can it be?"

"So you have to keep up the pace, plow as we go, follow the exodus," I said. "That's the price you were talking about."

"Not exactly," Don replied.

"What do you mean?" I asked. "What other big price to pay could there be?"

Don didn't answer verbally. He peered up to the rearview mirror, and just when I noticed he did that, the back door opened.

"Hi, everyone!" A young woman in her early twenties spoke in a chipper voice as she slid in. She wore a really nice ski jacket and a knit tousle cap with a big ball on top. "Whew!" she exhaled.

She had a really pretty face and actually wore makeup. I didn't get that. Did she actually take time to make up her face? Why?

"I'm ready." She faced Helen, took off her glove and extended her hand. "Jane."

"Jane?" Helen asked. "That's a very old-fashioned name."

"I'm an old-fashioned girl."

"Somehow, I doubt that."

She shook my hand and then sat back. "I'm ready, plow driver John."

"Don," he corrected.

"Don." She giggled. "Whoops. Road trip."

I peered at Don and spoke low. "That is the price to pay?"

"Yes."

I scoffed a laugh and said, "Okay," sitting back as he prepared to drive off.

Plowing the roads, staying in the back and going slowly, that was a price to pay. Giving Jane a ride, really, how bad could it be?

<><><><>

There was no cutting through the snow like a champ. For twenty minutes, the snow stopped, the sun freakishly shined, adding a slightly melted topping to the snow. Then the temperature took a nosedive and instantly everything froze.

The cars made the mistake of staying too close together, and because of where we were in the middle, we watched cars and trucks slip and slide, colliding into one another.

Each collision was a stop for someone to help. Not just us, others did too.

Don tried, like others, to plow, but for a good ten miles, until the snow built up again, the metal of the plow sounded more like it was scraping the concrete and it vibrated the truck as we went. Only slowly, very slowly.

I started to believe Don totally exaggerated in his implications about our new passenger. Maybe he didn't have the patience for the slightly post-teen girl. I didn't know much about her, but she wasn't that bad after her initial bright and cheery entrance into the truck. Then again, the first few upbeat moments were like a live version of the old blonde jokes.

She just didn't seem too bright. That was confirmed when she told us, "I can't believe it's winter already, it seems like we didn't even have a summer. Boy does time fly."

Yep.

I just forced a closed-mouth smile and agreed with her.

We didn't deal with her too long. She passed right out after a few minutes and a sip of brandy from Helen.

"Do you know what the plan is, Don?" Helen asked from the back seat.

"What do you mean?" he questioned.

"I mean, since you're helping, I thought maybe they told you the road plan. Obviously, they're trying to keep travelers together."

"Why do you suppose that is?" I asked Helen.

"Less stragglers, less death." She shrugged. "Don?"

"Yes, I did hear some things. They say once we hit South Carolina, the snow is far less, and in Georgia it's only an inch, but cold. Then again, they say we're getting another storm."

"Whoever 'they' are," I said. "Did they say what happened?"

Don shook his head. "Everyone can guess. No one really knows. We are stopping in a hundred miles. A relocation stop, picking up the workers there."

"A stop?" I asked. "You mean like where we were last night?"

"I believe so."

"I can ask about Glen and the kids," I said.

"Or," Helen added, "that Bob Abbot."

"They knew him at the camp last night," I said. "You're right. Maybe they know him, too."

"Then after that," Don said, "we stop at Washington, D.C."

"So, what gives with the snow bunny?" Helen asked with a point. "How did we end up with her and why was she a price to pay for this plow?"

"I recognized her," Don replied. "She then told Captain Holland she felt safe with me."

"You know her?" I asked.

"No. Not at all. I recognized her. I asked if she was the Vice President's daughter."

"Wait. Stop." I lifted my hand. "I don't even think I could recognize the Vice President let alone his daughter, and I'm from the US and you're not."

"And that is why," Don said. "We pay more attention."

"That's just crazy," I said.

Just then, a loud, long yawn emerged from the back seat.

I looked back there to see Jane stretching her arms. "Are we there yet?" she asked sleepily.

"Not yet," Don answered.

"Where is there?" I asked.

"D.C.," Jane answered. "But we need to get there in three days or else I'll miss my ride."

"So she's why we're going to D.C.?" I questioned. "What is she talking about, a ride?"

"Her father is still there," Don replied. "There is an evacuation supposed to be happening by air in three days."

"I'm sorry, but…" Again, I looked at Jane. "Why weren't you there in the first place?"

"I'm in school. I go to Yale."

"Yale. You go to Yale?" I asked. "How did you get into Yale?"

"I don't know," she said. "Some people are just lucky."

Helen laughed and mimed *Ha* then said, "Yes, I'm sure. Didn't you have a ride out of there? I mean if your dad is the VP, surely he arranged a ride?"

"Oh, he did, I missed it. I was doing clinicals. My last one. I couldn't miss it."

"Clinicals as in you're gonna be a nurse?" I asked.

Jane nodded. "I have to pass the test. Hopefully this time I will. The other two programs were fine, but I couldn't pass the test."

"Other two?" Helen asked.

"Nursing schools," Jane said. "Finally, Daddy said, go to Yale and if they can't make you pass the nurse test…"

"State boards," Helen corrected.

"Um, yes. I have to take those and pass. Between you and me I don't think I will."

"Unless your dad pays for it," Helen said.

"Wouldn't that be nice." Jane smiled. "Anyhow, I kept missing the ride, next thing I know I'm being bounced from one military ride to another. A week now. Boy, I'll tell you I felt like I was waiting to be in an usso show."

Don did a double take looking into the rearview mirror. "I'm sorry, a what?"

"An usso show," Jane repeated. "You know, famous singers and dancers perform for the troops, but I'm not a famous singer. I do karaoke well."

Helen groaned. "USO."

"Yes," Jane said. "Why do people spell it?"

"And they let you take care of sick people?" Helen quipped.

With an *Ah-hmm* she nodded, oblivious to the sarcasm. "Why are we stopping?"

"We're not," I said.

"We are now," Don added.

I felt the truck slow down and after looking at Jane for her odd prediction, I looked forward through the windshield. Everything had come to a grinding halt.

"What's going on?" I asked. No one was moving, the snow was falling, something was up.

I saw Captain Holland as he walked from the bus toward us, and waved for Don. He wasn't waving for me, I knew that. But like Don, I placed on my coat and opened my truck door.

"Oh! I'm coming too," Jane said brightly.

"Thank God," Helen grumbled.

"Are you coming?" Jane asked her.

"No, I'll stay here where it's warm."

Putting on my gloves, I closed the door and walked around to the front of the truck where Don stood.

I expected the captain to wait, but he had turned around and walked beyond the bus.

I suppose he wanted Don to follow him, and we did. Others did as well. They got out of their cars and slowly walked ahead.

I felt as if we were walking toward the edge of the earth. There was an inner anticipation, something was there, something was driving the curiosity and causing the captain to call for Don.

Maybe it was something as simple as a mound of snow and he was calling Don, the plow expert, for advice.

Slowly we walked, the wind blowing in our faces, heavy snow falling at a steady pace.

"The snow is so nice," Jane said.

Don and I both stopped and looked back at her.

"Don't you think?" she asked.

We started walking again and soon enough we emerged to the front of the buses where the lead plows had also stopped. Like the others, we edged our way past them to the road ahead and saw what caused everything to come to a grinding halt.

"Look how pretty," Jane commented.

"Pink snow," I said, looking at the two mounds that blocked the road.

They weren't large, maybe five feet in height and just as round in diameter. At the base and speckled around them the snow was pink.

"Pink snow," I repeated. "Algae causes that. Probably water that blew from the lake. I saw that on the Weather Channel. It's also called Watermelon snow."

"I know what you're talking about, but this isn't pink snow," Don said. "It's blood."

SIXTEEN

DEEP IN

When Aaron was six years old, Glen and I hit a bad spot. Bad was putting it mildly. He went through what I like to call a midlife crisis. Maybe because we were married so young; maybe I was too demanding. I didn't know. He needed space, needed to feel a little free and I tried so hard to understand that. I said nothing when he joined a dart league once a week. I thought it was a good idea. Meet new people. But the going out on Thursdays turned into two nights then three, pretty soon it was almost every night. Before it got to that point, Helen would tell me to rein him in. I just was fearful of doing so.

To me, Glen was trying to find some sort of happiness. He was trying to start a business and it was in the feast or famine stage, more famine than feast. But his partying ways brought on more famine. It seemed like every other week he was getting into a fight and the police got involved. Until one day, drinking, he rolled his car.

It was late and no one was on the road. He walked away without a scratch, but it could have been worse, much worse. Someone innocent could have been killed by his reckless behavior.

Did it teach him a lesson?

No. He started it again and after a year and a half, after several more run-ins with the police and fights, he got back on track.

Still, though, it scarred me in a strange way.

Any time I saw a police car zip by or pulling someone over, a twinge would hit my gut and I'd fear it was Glen.

Any accident or ambulance, I would hold my breath until I knew it wasn't him.

The pink snow was blood, blood that was so thick and plentiful it turned the bottom layer of snow into red ice. Each falling layer of snow absorbing a little blood until finally it was just pink instead of red. The victims had bled a lot. They were alive when the snow buried them. Laying there, hurt, no one to help.

The second I realized the pink snow was not a product of algae and the two mounds were cars from an accident, I immediately fell into old habits and assumed it was Glen and my children.

That panic, that dreaded thump to my gut, twisting and turning, I teetered on the verge of being unreasonable.

"Can we use the trucks to plow through?" Holland asked Don. "I mean, you're the expert."

"Just plow over?" Don question.

"Push it out of the way," Holland said.

"No. you can't do that. No." I raced forward to the pink snow, dropped to my knees and began to frantically uncover them.

"Mac, what are you doing?" Don rushed over.

"What if it's them?"

"What?"

"What if this is my family? What if it's them under this snow?"

"It's not."

"How do we know?" I asked emotionally.

"We don't until we look," Don said calmly joining me.

Jane stepped forward. "Should I try to help?"

"No," I replied, trying to dig through the hardened snow.

Don was the first to uncover a face. An older man, his expression peaceful, yet the entire side of his face was covered in blood. Don felt for a pulse, it was apparent he didn't find one. "This isn't Glen," he said.

"No, but what if it's Bob Abbot."

The expression on Don's face told me he wasn't arguing that. Soon our actions were contagious and, with at least a dozen people digging, following the pink snow, everything was uncovered.

Three victims. Both vehicles were overturned. Only one body remained in the car, the other two had been ejected.

We didn't know how far they'd rolled, how it happened. Don commented that it wasn't that difficult and despite how it seemed to be driving, there was very little control on the roads. One quick jerk was all that was needed. Small cars and top-heavy vehicles like mini vans and buses were more susceptible.

We cleared the road of the bodies and it was a lot more dignified than Holland's first suggestion of using the trucks to plow through and push everything aside.

Once I realized none of them were my family or Bob Abbot, I turned away. It was just another heart-wrenching loss I witnessed. No doubt, another of many.

"What happened?" Helen asked when we returned to the truck.

"An accident," I told her. "A bad one. No survivors."

Helen facially winced, then a look of sadness swept over her face. One that was replaced with a blank stare when Jane opened her mouth.

"If there were," Jane said, "I would have helped."

"I'm sure you would have." Helen patted her on her knee.

"I have the boo-boo bag."

"Isn't that nice," Helen said. "It's the thought that counts and I'm sure you'll get the chance."

The caravan of southbound, snow-driven vehicles rolled on.

I stared out the window as we passed the accident. Leaning close, my breathing caused a fog of condensation against the glass. I swiped it away.

The plow scattered more snow on the cars.

They would stay there, buried for no one knew how long.

Distance wise, it wasn't that far of a drive to Washington, D.C., maybe 150 miles. But the roads were snow covered and a steady but slow fall of fresh snow just complicated things.

A part of me, in the back of my mind, hoped that somehow we could get on that evacuation chopper. Get us south, get us to better weather so we could more easily look for my family.

But I knew that was a long shot.

That was if we even got there.

Instead of getting better the further south we went, it was worse. All I could hear was crunching and grinding under the wheels.

"I know Bob Abbot took I95," Don said. "That's what they told us, right? It's not smart."

"What do you mean?" I asked.

"I mean, as much as I want to follow their path. I want us to get to Georgia. Staying on 95 isn't going to do it. Any storm coming in from the ocean is going to be brutal. We need to move more inland."

"But we can't. You're plowing."

"I know," Don said. "They know we're taking Jane to D.C. I think after that, we make our break."

I understood where he was coming from and though I hated the thought of not being on the same road, I couldn't see a reasonable person, driving south, not thinking on the same lines as Don.

As we approached the relocation rest camp fifteen miles outside of Baltimore, we could see a chilling skyline of the city.

It was like something out of a sci-fi movie. The buildings were frosted over, at least it looked that way. We would get a better view once we took the beltway around the city.

The camp had dozens of tents and in the dismal day, only one was illuminated by a glowing orange.

The stop wasn't going to be long.

Four people were all we needed to pick up, and they weren't bringing anything but their personal belongings. Supplies would be left for if any travelers passed through. Removing the volunteers was for their safety.

We were supposed to just stay in our vehicles while the camp members loaded into Bus A, but I couldn't wait. I had to ask one of them about my family.

I zippered my coat and grabbed my phone, eyes peering out the windshield to the man talking to Holland.

"You're not gonna wait?" Don asked.

"No, what if we don't stop together?" I grabbed the door handle and opened it. Not surprising to me, Don followed.

I nearly fell the second my boot hit the ground. It looked soft, but the snow was rock hard. After slipping and getting my balance, carefully I walked to Bus A.

"Oh, hey," Holland said. "Glad you came out, Don, I need to ask you something. Your opinion since you're our plow expert."

It was like the third or fourth time I had heard that and it made me laugh internally. They all really looked at Don as some big guru on a plow and Don just went with it.

"Sure," Don said. "What's up?"

"This is Sam." Holland pointed with his head to a man. "He worked this camp and has some concerns."

"We got hit," Sam said. "I mean like really bad with some sort of freak freeze storm. Something you'd see in a movie. Froze everything instantly. We kept our woodburning stove roaring but all communications went down. That's why we weren't able to contact you. Anyhow, there's a small town, Taggert, small population, just about four miles up Route Six. They weren't evacuated and they won't be able to get to the main road. Six is covered. Is there a chance we can get them?"

"Plow a way?" Holland asked. "Is that possible, Don?"

"We can try," Don replied. "It's not that far. We can try. At the very least find out how many people need to be evacuated and wait."

Holland nodded. "We can leave Bus B behind. Radio ASAP when you get that intel, Don."

"Me?" Don asked.

"Well," I said, "why not? You are the plow expert."

"Exactly," Holland stated.

"We'll try," Don said. "That's the best I can do. We may not be able to reach them at all."

"Excellent. Not the not reaching them part," stated Holland. "I'll get people on Bus A, start the caravan, but we won't leave until we hear from you."

"Sam," I spoke up. "You been here a couple days at least. This is going to sound like a strange question, but do you know a man named Bob Abbot?"

139

"Bob, yeah," Sam said. "Always on the road."

"That's amazing," I commented. "Everyone seems to know him."

"None of us are military," Sam said. "We're all volunteers, we worked shops and stations along this road. So yeah, we know Bob. I remember when he did that episode of *Ice Road* something or other. Popped into my mind when I saw him yesterday. Hauling relocators."

"So he had people," I said. "I'm looking for my family." I pulled out the phone, swiped it once and as soon as I pulled up pictures, it died. "Shit. Damn it. I forgot to charge it in the truck."

"Maybe after you charge it," Holland told me. "Let me get Sam on the bus."

"But you saw Bob?" I asked. "And he had people with him. My mother-in-law and I got washed off a bridge in Pennsylvania."

"The folks he had were all from the bridge. He told me that. But to be honest," Sam said, "I didn't see who was in that deluxe road thing. I didn't. They didn't stop for long. An hour and they moved on." Sam started to walk to the bus.

"Did you see a teenage boy? A girl?"

"I didn't see who was in the vehicle, only Bob got out and got fuel." He took a few more steps away.

"Let's go." Don took my arm. "You can show him the pictures later."

"My husband was wearing an Eagles cap," I tried once more.

Sam stopped walking. He stared at me for a second.

"You saw him," I said.

"I did. We can talk when we stop." Sam said no more and walked to the front bus.

I spun to Don. "He saw him. The kids had to be in the truck, right?"

"Right."

"Don," Holland hollered. "We ready?"

"Yes. We're heading now." Don faced me. "Why don't you head back to the plow and I'll find out where I need to go."

"Just about now aren't you worried you won't live up to the title plow expert?"

"No, not at all."

And he probably wasn't.

I walked back to the truck, looking over my shoulder once more to see Don walking to the bus. Once back at the plow, I got inside.

"Anything?" Helen asked immediately.

"The man saw Glen."

"Oh." Helen exhaled, placing her hand on her chest. "They made it this far. I'm relieved."

I nodded. "Right now, though, we have to find some road and plow a way to a small town so they can get out."

"Are they leaving us behind?"

I shook my head. "No, some are going ahead. We'll radio once we get to the town to see if a bus has to wait. I'm not sure. Don is getting the information now. But this guy, Bob Abbot, is some sort of expert driver. Our family is in good hands."

"That's great news."

I quickly turned my head when the driver's door opened and Don got in.

"The turn to Route Six is a quarter mile down," Don explained. "Small community. Just waiting for a way to get out."

"Let's go get them."

It was easier said than done. Plow a road, clear a path, head to D.C. After all, that was the next stop.

141

Just before the quarter-mile mark where we'd find the turn to Route Six, Don had to lower the plow. Sam wasn't kidding or exaggerating when he said there was no way for them to get out.

No car or truck could possibly get through. Had we not known there was a road there, we would have passed it.

The side of the road was all snow, at least three feet high, and the only thing that made the road partially distinguishable was the break in the trees and the lone telephone pole.

We made the turn and slowly plowed forward.

Those poor people in Taggert. I could only imagine their desperation, how forgotten they had to feel.

We were already a country divided.

Those trying to find safety and those wishing we weren't.

We'd free them, cut them a route, and they, like us would be the nomads of a frozen world. Moving in hopes of something better.

But was there better out there?

Our short exodus had been hard thus far, and I couldn't imagine it would get any easier.

SEVENTEEN

SHELF LIFE

I had seen it once in a movie. Some over-budgeted, science-fiction thriller depicting the next ice age with flare and drama. At the time, Glen and I had laughed. The skeptic in him immediately going online and looking up facts.

"That would never happen," he ridiculed. "Look, Mac, look what this says."

Couldn't we just enjoy the movie? An escape from reality. Yet, there I was in the middle of that movie.

The only difference was there didn't seem to be a bright, beautiful sunrise on the horizon, and a huge rescue initiative that would bring us all together.

Something happened and they just stopped calling cities to evacuate.

They forgot about those of us up north.

The people of Taggert had to feel left behind. Radio communications had been cut, the road in and out of their town buried in hardened snow.

The closer we got to the small town, the harder it was to plow. Helen came up with the idea that if we couldn't get the people out, we had cleared the road enough that Bus B could get to them.

That was a choice, an option, until we saw that the people in Taggert had stopped waiting.

That revelation came in the form of a man. Knee-deep in the snow in the middle of the road, a shovel in his hand. He was nearly bent in half. The snow held his body up enough that when he'd collapsed, he never fell over.

"They were trying to dig their way out," Don said, opening the door.

"I'll go this time," Helen said, stepping out with Don.

"I got the boo-boo bag," Jane said. "Though I don't think it will help him." She, too, got out of the truck.

I didn't.

I couldn't.

I just couldn't look at another dead body. I didn't want to know if there were more out there or if he was the lone one.

I sat in the truck with no guilt at first about staying behind. I watched as the three of them looked at the man, then stared off beyond him before walking off. Once they disappeared into the snow, that guilt finally settled in.

What did they see that caused them to investigate?

I shut off the truck, grabbed the keys, and prepped my coat and hat to go outside. I hated it. It was cold and the snow burned as it hit my face with force. I could call for them but there was no way they would see me.

Arms tight to my body, I walked toward the snow where the man had found his final resting place.

His head was down, he wore a hat and it was hard to see his face. I didn't try, I only stepped forward to see what I could.

They'd tried to dig out. Probably banded together as a town and dug away. There were cars abandoned and snow-covered in the streets. From where I stood, I could see Don and Helen looking in cars, while Jane walked up to the shops that lined the streets.

They had a tough time walking in the snow. Bringing their knees high to take a step. They were yelling out something, but I couldn't make out what. They weren't yelling to me, of that I was sure.

I didn't need to be in the town to know one of two things had happened.

They were all dead or they were all gone.

With that on my mind, I returned to the truck.

They weren't gone long. Long enough for the truck to get cold again.

They all got back in. Helen verbally shivered, calling out, "Start it, Don. Please."

He did, then immediately picked up the radio. "Holland, come in."

A moment later the response came. "This is Holland, go."

"Taggert is...we looked. Not every building, but there were no signs of people. Can't say if some aren't in their homes, but there was no smoke from fires. We did see signs that they walked."

"They walked?" Holland asked.

"Looks like they tried to dig out, couldn't and some, if not a lot, walked."

"Where would they go?" Holland asked.

"I don't know."

"Okay, we'll head out. Catch you on the highway. Over."

"Out." Don replaced the receiver to the truck radio.

"Did they really walk?" I asked.

"Yes." Don put the truck in reverse and cautiously attempted a three-point turn. It took a good five minutes, inching forward, then back.

"How do you know?" I asked. "I mean, wouldn't the snow have covered the tracks?"

"Some of them…" Don looked at me. "Didn't make it that far."

A sickening knot hit my gut. I slid down in my seat, exhaling slowly through my partially parted lips.

"It looked," Helen said, "as if they died in the middle of what they were doing. Walking, digging."

My eyes cast to the rearview mirror and to the man that was in the snow. "How is that even possible?" I murmured.

Don must have heard me. I didn't expect an answer, but he was willing to offer one. "Sam said a freak cold blew in."

Helen added, "The cold causes your blood vessels to constrict and narrow. That's why they tell people with heart conditions not to shovel. Cold and exertion causes heart attacks. I think, and this is just my opinion, it was so cold it caused their hearts to stop, lungs to freeze."

Don looked up to the rearview mirror. "Jane, you're a health professional. You went all the way through nursing school…"

"Three times."

"Yes," he said. "What do you think?"

"I agree."

I silently huffed shaking my head and peered out my window. Why would he even ask her? She was as much a health professional as he was a professional plow driver. She had a 'boo-boo' bag for crying out loud. Besides, we didn't need a health professional to tell us what happened. We would never know what killed those people, where the others went or if they were alive or dead.

There would be no investigation, no one to care.

The mystery of the town of Taggert would forever be just that…a mystery.

<><><><><>

From a distance Baltimore looked frozen and as we moved closer to the city, it looked as if God Himself had taken a can of white spray paint and sprayed every building, road, and bridge.

It looked fake. But it wasn't.

We weren't far behind the caravan at all. Several cars were behind us as we took 195 through the city. The beltway was out of the question because to loop around the city we needed to go through the Baltimore Harbor Tunnel. Radio chatter confirmed that no one wanted to take a chance in case the tunnel was jam-packed. Instead, led by two larger plows, we moved slowly down the highway which crossed the Patapsco River. As frightening as it was, the site was beautiful. The river and the harbor were completely frozen over. The wind whipped up the snow close to the surface of the river, creating mini cyclones.

Don was right. The water brought in the cold.

The highway through the city was mostly overpasses covering secondary city streets and even a railyard. It was evident the roads had been plowed before the previous night's snow. They were frozen over, causing us to move even more slowly.

The lead plows created blusters of snow that caught the wind and carried over to the side of the road.

There was a defeated silence in our truck. A simple task of plowing an escape for a small town hadn't been so simple and ended up being a tragic failure.

We didn't speak, all of us just watching ahead.

I felt like I was holding my breath. Wanting to get off those dangerous overpasses and out of the city. The sky grew more gray as the dark clouds built up, summoning yet another round of heavy winter weather.

It was getting dark. We had little daylight hours and I knew, even though we were so close to Washington, D.C., there was no way we would make it before nightfall. The entire caravan would have to stop for the night.

There were no camps up ahead, none that we were told about anyway.

Every exit we passed, I wanted us to just get off the highway and to the roads below where we weren't supported by frozen concrete high above the ground.

It was unfounded nervousness.

Jane suddenly wheezed out a breath and called out to Don, "Stop."

Was she sick? Maybe going to throw up? I dismissed her and looked out the window as we passed the exit that advertised a plethora of take out. Knowing our flighty passenger she probably thought she could get a take-out burger.

"Dan," she said.

"Don," he corrected.

"Please stop."

"Why do you want me to…?"

"Stop!" she yelled. "Stop. Stop! Now!"

"Alright," Don replied calmly. He turned on the hazard lights and slowly brought us to a stop.

I was certain the cars behind us weren't happy, especially as the rest of the caravan moved ahead.

"Okay, we stopped," Don said. "Why?"

"I don't know. I had a feeling," Jane replied.

Just as I started to roll my eyes in ridicule and irritation, it happened.

Boom.

It took my breath away.

I had never heard anything so loud or felt anything like it. An intense vibration that shook my core and caused a buzzing in my ears. The overpass swayed with the shaking, causing the truck to slide sideways across the road.

"Don!" I shrieked.

He grabbed the wheel, trying to control it when another loud boom rang out. This time I saw it. A huge plume of white mist shot up like a geyser from below the highway. But it wasn't mist, it was ice, and the frozen debris rained down upon the road. Just as it settled, another burst occurred, then another.

If I hadn't known better, I would have sworn they were some sort of ice volcanos.

The road buckled. Don swerved diligently attempting to command the truck. I clutched one hand to the dash, the other to the 'oh shit' bar, praying in my head it would stop.

It didn't

The earth quaked more violently. Ahead of us the caravan of cars became a jumbled mess. They went back and forth, hitting each other, and as the final expulsion rang out, the section of the overpass ahead collapsed, taking with it every vehicle that was on it.

They all tumbled and slid to the ground below. One right after another, fast and furiously. A huge billow of snow erupted creating a huge cloud and it rolled our way.

The usually mild-mannered Don blurted out an uncharacteristic and slightly concerned, "Son of a bitch," as he threw the truck into reverse and slammed the gas.

We spun backwards. Cars behind us be damned and I didn't realize why until I saw what he must have seen first.

The entire overpass ahead of us was collapsing, inch by inch, foot by foot, coming our way.

The truck spun in a circle until he finally faced us the opposite way. I didn't look ahead, I looked behind, as did Jane and Helen.

I could feel the tires spinning in our getaway and watched as nature gobbled up the road, giving us no choice but to get off the highway or parish.

Despite our attempts to move forward, the ground didn't stop shaking.

Finally, I turned around, no longer wanting to see how close things were. I couldn't figure out how Don could even see. We moved as fast as we could, the plow still pushing snow and sending it up into the windshield. Panicked, I looked in the side mirror for the cars that were behind us. Were they okay? I didn't feel us hit them.

I wondered if they'd dropped below. It was so close.

I put my faith in Don.

With what I believed as a wing and prayer, Don jerked the wheel hard and we veered to the right.

Please let there be a ramp there. Please.

The truck bounced hard once, I heard the plow slam down and, still on four wheels we all but glided down the exit ramp.

His eyes went from rearview to side-view mirror, continuously driving, creating distance.

Finally, at what I hoped was a good distance, he spun the truck again in an attempt to stop. Three cars sped by us and stopped. The ground wasn't moving, but it wasn't over.

Like the weather, we all froze staring outward watching as the entire supported highway crumbled down.

EIGHTEEN

SIMMER

To say we were fortunate was an understatement. We were also so focused on that collapsing roadway we didn't see how much damage was done to Baltimore.

The wreckage was massive. It was hard to distinguish where one car ended and a piece of the overpass began.

We all stood there, staring at the humongous, tangled mess, steam rising up from the warm vehicles pressed against the cold. Some of the engines were still running, I could hear that.

My heart still raced and I fought to calm it down.

"What was that?" Helen asked.

"Felt like an earthquake," Don answered. "At least to me."

"Maybe it was an ice quake," Jane suggested. "I heard that term before."

Don shook his head. "Usually they occur when the ground is frozen and the temperature warms up too much. But it definitely is related to the weather."

"The ice geysers," I said.

We began to move toward the wreckage. I was shocked to see the others getting back in their car.

"You guys need to get out of here," one man yelled. "This is not safe. It happened once, it will happen again. You won't be so lucky."

"We need to look for survivors," Don replied.

"No one survived that," another man said.

He was right, at least I felt that. But we had to look. It wasn't like we could do anything for the injured, but was it better than dying and being buried alive.

The other cars left.

It wouldn't be long before it was dark. Not only would we have to forfeit the search, we also had to find shelter, we had to get away from the city.

It truly was dangerous.

Once again, no one spoke. It was so quiet. An occasional engine noise, a sputter of exhaust sound. I couldn't help but credit the town of Taggert for our survival. Had we not gone to get them, we would have been there with the others, twisted into the rubble.

A portion of one of the buses protruded out.

It was right then that it became real. Not a scene from a movie or hand-painted drawing.

"My God, Don, there are children on those buses. In those cars."

"I know." He moved forward, all of us did.

I didn't even know where to begin. We called out to people, then stopped and waited to see if we heard anything. A cry…a whimper.

We didn't hear a sound.

It was a layered mess of destruction. Cars, concrete, broken windows, a body part here and there.

It created an emotion in my gut that just made me want to scream.

How was it possible?

Almost every person trying to get out and go south, every person in our caravan was dead. They thought the safest way was to stay together, two plows up front leading the way, the buses with plows, all together.

But it was their downfall.

How many would have lived if they would have just moved at their own pace?

It was no one's fault. Nature was lashing out, but as far as I was concerned it was only aimed at those of us in the north.

Baltimore was a frozen, dangerous mess. The wind picked up, the snow blew harder, and the sky grew increasingly dark.

We were outside so long, my face was frozen and I couldn't feel my lips. My gut instinct told me there were people alive in that mound, there had to be.

The problem was, we just didn't have the luxury of time to find them.

We needed to get out of the city and find shelter.

I felt heartbroken. I hated giving up, we all did.

But we had to go. We had to move. We had to stay alive.

<><><><>

"We can't be dumb the next time," Helen said. "Or else we'll die. We can't run on emotions. We have to think."

Once we'd stopped for the evening, Helen went exploring, getting items, gathering supplies. I didn't know how she could even think of that. I was distraught. I just wanted to stop and cry.

The weather worked in our favor and we made it a little farther than I believed we would. We pulled over at a hotel just off the highway. One long since shut down, probably when everything started to change.

There was a fireplace in the lobby and Don broke furniture to get enough wood to get it started. It was dark and we used the small oil candles from the restaurant tables to give us light.

We were there for the night, at least twelve hours.

Jane disappeared too immediately upon our arrival. I thought they went through the hotel. There was a lot there. A restaurant, a bar…kitchen. But instead they went across the road to the Food Giant and picked up supplies.

"When I was a young girl, and after I had my son, my mother told me to wrap something called Sarin Wrap around my belly. The plastic holds in heat." She passed them out. "Should we be outside, you will have them under your socks, on your hands, everywhere we can. We're at the point we may need to walk. It's coming. I feel it."

"I agree," Don said. "We need to prepare for walking."

"How far from Washington are we?" I asked.

"Thirty miles, maybe a little more," Don replied.

It was warm by the fire; I no longer shivered. Even with the heat in the truck, I just couldn't warm up after standing outside so long in the rubble.

Jane handed me a small tube. "Here. For your lips."

My lips.

I hadn't even thought about it, but when she handed me the ointment, I reached up to feel them. They were swollen and sore. I could feel the blisters already forming on them.

"Thank you," I said.

"It was heartbreaking today," Jane said. "All those people. Those poor people."

I had this void in me. This dead space. An ache that told me that we just gave up too soon, that we left people to die. Every time I thought about that collapse, I thought about all those people. Families I had seen in the food line.

The workers that had joined us.

Sam…the man who had the answers about my family, the man who'd told me he would talk to me later…gone.

I felt horrible and guilty. All that, combined with the worry about my family, was an emotional knot I couldn't undo.

Helen sorted the supplies she had found, she seemed so oblivious and strong. She gathered blankets from the beds—pillows, towels. She found a lot of things, I wondered how we would carry them if indeed we had to walk like she had said.

She focused on those items.

On one hand I envied her; on the other I was angry. Glen was her son, my children were her grandchildren. Wasn't she distraught? Worried? She barely showed it.

Don was an anomaly. He didn't show emotions at all. Calm and quiet.

Jane went through phases. Chatty Kathy one moment and silent the next.

Helen had found a large can of tomato soup in the kitchen. It took almost an hour to warm it to a steaming point. We dined on that with crackers and peanut butter, and shared a bottle we took from the hotel bar.

Before I had even finished my meal, I could feel the effects of the cold on my lips. It burned to take a drink or let the soup pass into my mouth. I ended up consuming both with a straw.

Everyone fell asleep long before me. My mind couldn't stop thinking and my stomach was nauseous. Probably from the odd combo of food and drink we'd consumed.

Outside, the glow of the fire and tiny candles created a ring of darkness surrounding us in the lobby.

Alone and awake I wondered about the people in the community and town. Where were they all? Had they made a mad dash for the south, were they dead?

The world had suddenly become a very scary place, one I increasingly grew frightened of.

A world I had denied would happen was beating at me.

Blanket wrapped around my shoulders, I wandered from the semi-lit area into the darkness toward the long wall of glass windows in the lobby.

I couldn't see anything out there. It was black, completely and utterly black. No distant lights, no moon.

I couldn't see if it was snowing, or had it stopped?

It was a reflection of what I was feeling: a dark void of complete uncertainty.

I thought of Glen, was he standing by a window like me looking out? Cleo was always such a fussy eater, was she eating anything? And Aaron, he was still healing from his injuries just a few days beforehand. Was he alright? Was he better?

For all I knew, my children witnessed what they thought was my death. They had to believe me to be dead.

The anguish and hurt they had to be feeling.

They were traveling in the world probably with no care about a destination in Georgia now, just trying to move, get south, stay alive, mourn their mother and grandmother.

I realized as I stood by that window that me and my family were on the same journey.

The same road. The same direction.

They were forging ahead, trying to find a way to live.

I was forging ahead, trying to find them so I could live. Without them in my life, with the world the way it was, cold and dangerous, there was no reason to stay alive.

NINETEEN

BEAR

August 5

My head was pounding, probably from exhaustion and sadness. I sat on the floor, leaning my head against the cold glass of the lobby windows; that was where I fell asleep, though not where I woke up.

I knew immediately upon opening my eyes that someone had moved me. I sat up in a startle.

"Morning," Helen said.

"Am I the last one up?" I asked.

"You are."

"How did I get here?"

Helen opened her mouth to answer, but Jane did.

"Don," Jane replied. "I just made a coffee. Would you like it?" She extended the cup.

"I don't want to take yours," I said.

"There's more. Take it. Did you want some oatmeal?" She handed me her cup then reached to her backpack. "Look at these cute little single servings. I took a bunch."

"Oatmeal is good for the soul," Helen said. "Will keep you going all day. And those are instant. We have snow, so we have water. Just let them sit."

"I'll pass on the oatmeal," I said. "I'm not really hungry. The coffee will work, thank you." I brought the cup to my lips, sipped and cringed. "I forgot how sore they were."

"Straw." Jane handed me one. "Use it."

"Thank you."

"So," Helen said. "How did you end up passed out at the window. Were you drunk?"

I shook my head. "I was staring out. I had a headache. I rested against it and fell asleep." My eyes shifted around. All the bags were packed. "When were you guys planning on waking me?'

"Soon," Helen replied. "At least with enough time to wake up and wash up if you want."

"I need that…" My eyes gazed up to a loud thump.

Don walked toward us dropping something on the floor. "Done. It's about twenty-five pounds."

"Don, again," Helen said, "I'm impressed."

I couldn't figure out what it was. It was about two and a half feet tall with a metal frame. Tied to it were four blankets tightly rolled. "What is it?"

"It's a blanket holder," Jane said.

Don chuckled. "Not really. I found it in the back. It's a cot. An emergency cot. But like I told Helen when I went looking, I wanted to find something we could use as a sled to carry our things if we have to walk. And this is perfect."

Jane gasped loudly. "Oh wow! That's a super cool idea. That's because you're from Canada. You probably know a lot of Eskimo."

Don looked at her quickly. At first I thought he was offended, then I realized he was just shocked by her response. "No," he told her, "I don't. But living in Canada, where I'm from, that did give me the sled idea."

"Very good idea," I said.

"We have a lot of things between us. Stuff I would hate to leave behind. This will work well. I'm going to put this and the rest of our stuff in the truck. I'd like to get going soon."

Of course, he did. We all did. We weren't all that far from Washington, D.C., though where in D.C. we had to go was still to be determined. Jane hadn't told us.

I helped Don get the things into the truck and couldn't believe the weather had been kind. Very little snow had fallen, but I wasn't holding out hope it would stay snow-free, the sky was too dark and I could smell it coming in the air.

We loaded up and left. Once we hit the highway there were tire tracks. They weren't deep and by the looks of them, the person wasn't having an easy time driving, but they were fresh.

Four miles down the road, we spotted a blue pickup truck. Snow was impacted in the wheels and it only had a dusting of snow on it.

Whoever was driving, was now on foot.

"We need to keep an eye out," I said. "Look for these people." Finding them, helping them was important to me. We failed those on the overpass, we could at least look and try to help those walking.

Time was running out.

It didn't take long for the snow to start falling again, only this time it was heavy and fast. The wind whipped up and I could feel it moving the truck.

I could also feel the strain on the plow.

The snow piled up faster than it had been, so fast that had we not known to look for someone walking, I would have sworn the moving figure was a bear. The person had a large hunch to their back and was completely covered with snow.

"There." I pointed. "See him. Only one person."

"I see him." Don honked the horn. He didn't hear us. The wind had to be loud out there.

Finally, we caught up to him, slowing down before we arrived. It was a man, and the hunch on his back was a backpack. He did a double take, stopped, and raced to us.

I would say he was glad we pulled over.

His face was buried beneath a ski mask which was completely covered with snow. He wore shaded googles that I could tell he kept swiping to clear snow.

"Get in," Don said.

Helen opened up the back door and he stepped inside.

"I don't know how long we'll keep going," Don said. "I'm pushing the plow as it is right now."

"Any distance," he replied. "I just need to get warm, Don, thank you."

Don? Did he say Don?

I hurriedly looked back at him as he took off his hat and googles.

It was Captain Holland.

His nose was swollen, and his eyes bruised, otherwise he said he was fine.

"Do you want me to help you?" Jane asked him.

Holland was quick to turn her down, not before showing a brief look of panic at the prospect of Jane tending to his wounds.

I was happy to see he'd survived, yet, overwhelmed with guilt that he was alive and we had just left. That somehow he'd been alone out there while we were tucked away in a hotel lobby with a warm, raging fire.

I told him I was sorry.

"You can't feel that way," he told us. "I didn't regain consciousness until it was dark. The only thing that kept me from freezing to death was all the bodies on me." He lowered his head for a moment. "I found a truck. And it started. I knew I wouldn't get far but I had to try."

"Was there anyone else alive?" Don asked.

"Not that I saw. It was bad."

"You're alive." Helen tapped his leg. "And warming up?"

"Yes, ma'am. Thank you."

His color started to normalize showing his bruising even more. It was a good thing he did warm up, because it wasn't long before the highway and weather finally got the best of us.

The wheels of the truck spun without making much progress forward, the gears were grinding, and the plow sounded like a dying cat.

Don pushed it as hard and as far as he could, getting every inch out of the road that he could. The plow wasn't battling snow, it was battling ice we couldn't break through.

Finally, he conceded.

We had been lucky. We'd had a good run. Better than most. But shortly after the 'Fifteen miles to Washington' sign, our luck ran out.

We had no choice but to get ready and walk.

TWENTY

ACROSS THE WAY

It wasn't for lack of trying. Don did try backing up and going at it again, but nothing. It seemed to be a wall blocking us from driving any farther.

Before leaving, we prepared…Helen style.

She passed out the plastic bags for our feet and hands and we stayed in the warm truck while Don and Holland put together our emergency cot sleigh.

Don knew it was coming. He'd built that sled because he knew we'd have to venture on foot eventually.

Before all of this, Holland attempted to radio again. He had lost contact with the two soldiers with the vice president. He wouldn't have worried about that as much, chalking it up to lost communication due to the weather, had he not been able to reach the station base in Richmond. That base was supposed to be the relay stopping point after the vice president was airlifted.

They, too, had not spoken with the vice president.

The last Holland had spoken, they were moving not only to high ground, but accommodations conducive to surviving and being air lifted.

He never learned that destination. He didn't know if the vice president had even arrived.

"We'll find him," Jane kept saying. "I have faith. I mean it's Washington, D.C., how hard could it be?"

Who was I to dampen her hopes or shoot them down? I was looking for my family as well.

We had stayed in the warm truck long enough.

Holland gave us instructions before we left. "Don't look into the wind, try not to moisten your lips and do no not talk unless you absolutely have to. Keep the air out of your lungs as much as possible."

Keeping the air out of our lungs was easier said than done. We did have to breathe.

We left the truck. The snow was firm and frozen enough to walk on, but not enough to support the weight of the truck. It was like climbing a hill to continue on the highway. The plows had stopped days before when D.C. was evacuated.

Don and Holland each carried an end of the rope, pulling the sled of supplies, while Helen, Jane, and I followed behind.

They wanted to make sure there were no weak spots in the snow. We followed their footsteps. If someone was going to fall through, they would.

Once we got into Washington, D.C., we'd have to try to figure out where the vice president was.

We had fifteen miles before we reached the city limits.

With the weather as bad as it was, it might as well have been a hundred miles.

<><><><>

165

"Don't look into the wind," was the best advice I had been given. I just wish I had listened and followed it or, at the very least, lowered the visor on my plastic bonnet to shield my eyes.

The wind made my eyes water and not long after, my eyelashes became iced over and snow gathered on my face. I couldn't see and it burned.

Our first stop was earlier than anticipated, mainly because of me. We stopped at a convenience store gas station and had to break the windows to get in. The snow had piled up four feet and we couldn't access the doors.

I was glad it was August because they had sunglasses. I would use them to shield my eyes and everyone grabbed a pair.

We sat down inside, long enough to take the chill off. It felt warm in there, but it wasn't. It was just so cold outside.

I was a hot mess and wanted Don to fire up that Fury 4400 Kerosene heater, but knew it was a lot of trouble to undo it from the sled. Plus, we would need it when we stopped for the night.

While there, even for half an hour, I did what I always did when we stopped, I pulled out Cleo's little boot and held it in my hand.

"Look what I found," Helen said, showing me a bottle. "Now I know alcohol isn't good when you're cold, but a little swig won't hurt."

"Thank you." I took the bottle

She handed me a straw.

I merely gave a glance of gratitude, took the straw, placed it in the bottle and took a sip.

"How are you doing?" Helen asked.

"Not as well as you."

"Well, years as a crossing guard really prepared me for this."

"So says the woman who wore a sweater in eighty-degree weather."

"I never had much tolerance for the cooler weather," Helen said. "I was always cold. I think that's why this isn't bothering me as much. Same will happen to you."

"I doubt it. I doubt I'll even make it through this," I told her. "And it isn't just the weather, it's what is happening. You have to be humane or tough as nails. Be able to walk away or put your own needs aside to help. I don't have either in me and I'm not that nice of a person who people will want to help."

"You have your moments." Helen reached out and tapped my hand.

"Gee, thanks."

"I blame your job. I told you the day you accepted that position it was going to make you hard. Not tough, hard. You hear so many sob stories you become immune to them. Like when a nurse sees a lot of death. You, you saw a lot of people's bullshit."

I lowered my head. "I did."

"That's a hard habit to break. Thinking everyone is handing you a line. Just like it was a hard habit for me to believe everyone was innocent like the kids. You'll make it through this. I'll make sure of it. Because I promise we will all be together again."

I lifted my eyes, looking around. First at Holland, then Don, and finally Jane. I leaned into Helen, whispering, "We don't know where her father is or even if…he's alive."

"I know."

"Do you think she knows it might not happen?"

"Sure," Helen said. "Sure she does. But she's staying positive. She made it this far when she couldn't even get a ride. I think that girl has blind luck. So, bet me that will lead us to her dad."

"Maybe even a ride south," I said.

"Hmm."

"What? What's with that?"

"It's a chopper. I don't know with this weather. We may be safer taking our chances walking."

"I'm sure they have the best pilots. And that's even if they let us on the chopper. They may not."

"That's true. Maybe the captain will help us. Do we even know his first name?"

I shook my head. "Surprisingly, I think we know the most about Jane. I mean, we don't even know Don's story. Other than he's a teacher, does speaking, and was headed south. I mean is there more?"

Don cleared his throat. Obviously, he could hear us and was paying attention. "All you have to do is ask."

"Okay," Helen said. "What's your story, Don?"

"I'm a teacher, I do speaking, and I was headed south."

"That's it?" Helen asked.

"That's it. That and I'm from Canada."

"No life tragedy? No back story, perhaps a criminal murderous past you're hiding?"

"Nope."

Jane giggled. "You guys are funny. Like he would tell you if he did. Silly." She shook her head. "Is everyone feeling alright?" she asked. "Anyone need me to check them?"

We all answered with a very quick, "No."

"Mac, do you need me to check your eyes and lips?"

"I'm good. Thank you. Helen is on it."

"Okay. Just let me know. I am certain I have something in the boo-boo bag."

168

"I'll keep that in mind," I said politely. Even though I wanted to know why she mentioned my eyes, I refrained because any conversation with her would bring about something being said that wasn't quite so bright.

We stayed in that store for a little bit longer. Helen was slightly disappointed when it didn't have adult beverages on the shelves.

Holland had to inform her that Maryland had some strict liquor laws and then as we left, he told us his first name was Dennis.

Many times during our walk, my mind traveled back to my younger days when we used to have heavy snow. Like eating watermelon will trigger a summer feeling, hearing the wind and the brightness of the blanketed snow, along with the frigid air that found its way through every layer of covering I wore reminded me of those days from my childhood.

It brought it all back.

When I hadn't a care in the world how long I was outside, or how cold my nose and feet would get. Warmth was a short distance away with a cup of something warm to drink.

I didn't often look back on my youth. So much of it was a blur. The early years were a long-forgotten memory.

I never knew my parents; they died when I was really young. No one from my biological family ever stepped forward to take care of me. I never knew if I had any. I thought of looking for them when I got old enough but ditched that idea. If they were out there, they never looked for me.

I was fortunate. Even though I was in the system I always had good foster parents. Even the ones that did it as a job weren't bad. I was never hungry or mistreated. I didn't have the horror stories some of the kids did.

My last set of foster parents were an older couple and it was through their church I met Glen. When the county removed me from services I was placed in transition housing at eighteen. They stayed close for a while but then drifted as their biological children seemed to inch me out.

I often wondered if I latched onto Glen so strongly because of his parents. His father especially. Glen's dad was an amazing man; Helen seemed to tolerate me.

She still tolerated me to this day. Although she kept me going on our walk, I felt useless. Never able to keep my footing, I moved awkwardly and slow. The cold beat at me, making my body hurt, my lips could barely part, and my eyes burned so badly I wanted to cry, not that I could have.

I paled in comparison to the strength and fortitude of a seventy-four-year-old woman.

She put me to shame.

Even Jane…put me to shame.

The walk was quiet, it was impossible to talk, and Don and Holland used hand signals to let us know we were stopping and taking a break.

The frequent breaks kept us going and moving a lot farther than I thought we would.

As the sky started to darken, we stopped for the night, finding another hotel just on the edge of the Washington, D.C. limits. There was no way we would make any headway inside D.C., not as evening crept up.

I thought maybe it was a comfort thing or habit that Don found a hotel.

It was a big one, at least ten stories high. The snow came halfway to the front doors which were plastered with signs that said the business was closed during the crisis.

Holland broke in through a side ballroom window and cleared a way for us to make our way in.

The hotel was dark and cold, and it didn't have a fireplace.

We set up camp for the night in a small meeting room just off the lobby, using candles for light and the Fury 4400 kerosene power blower for warmth.

It more than did the trick. It dried our clothes and created a toasty warm environment. It felt good to shed the layers and be dry. We didn't even need to keep it running constantly, only turning it on when it got too cold.

Helen found more bottles. I had never known her to be a big drinker. Maybe she was and I'd just never seen it, but she was in her glory after finding something in the bar.

Perhaps her strength wasn't a natural one but one she got from the bottle.

I was exhausted. I didn't want to move, but I wasn't sleepy, just worn out.

The next day would be tough. How were we even supposed to begin to find Jane's family?

It would take a miracle or blind luck. Which she claimed she had.

We were only in the beginning of this new frozen world, and I felt like I was at the end. Not a muscle in my body didn't hurt, I couldn't eat right because of the cold exposure to my eyes. They burned and I felt like I had pink eye. It was hard to keep them open.

Jane found some eye drops in the gift shop that worked, but I had to keep using them for any relief, at least until I fell asleep.

I would have thought for as much as we walked in silence we would have spoken to each other while in that room. No one did. Holland and Don kept leaving, I guessed to look for items that would be useful for our survival.

I wanted to scavenge through the hotel as well, but I just didn't have it in me.

Maybe if I had eaten. I was so hungry, but while everyone else dined on canned beef stew and peanut butter sandwiches, I sipped lukewarm tomato soup through a straw.

After everyone started to go to sleep, I absorbed the silence, sitting with my back against a wall. With Cleo's boot in my hand I closed my eyes thinking about my life, hoping I would drift off into sleep.

"Hey," Don said softly, giving me a soft shake. "I know you're not sleeping."

"I'm not," I said.

"You wanna see something?"

Just that question piqued my curiosity. I opened my eyes.

"Come on." He held out his hand to help me up.

I took it and stood.

"Grab your coat."

"Oh, please don't tell me we're going outside."

"We're going outside."

I groaned.

"Don't whine. You don't need to layer. Just the coat."

I grabbed my coat and put it on.

He motioned his head toward the door, walked that way and I followed.

He opened the door only slightly so as not to let the warmth out. The second I stepped into the pitch-black hall, the temperature was drastically colder.

He turned on the flashlight. "Follow me."

"Of course."

He took me to a stairwell.

"Seriously?" I asked. "It's dark in there."

"Your eyes will adjust."

"My eyes suck."

"Your corneas are just inflamed from the wind. Like wind burn. It'll get better," Don said.

"I hope. Or else I may have to turn to Jane."

Don laughed. I believe it was the first time I'd heard him make a laughing sound. We went into the stairwell and began to climb.

"How far up?" I asked.

"All the way."

"Oh my God, you have to be kidding."

"You just walked fifteen miles in the snow. You can do ten flights of stairs."

"No," I said. "I can't."

"You can."

I tried. A few flights up I had to stop. Then after another flight I stopped again to catch my breath. My legs felt like jelly.

Don didn't seem irritated. In fact, he was patient with me.

"I don't think those fifteen miles did anything for me," I said.

"You'll see. In a short time you'll be in great shape."

"In a short time I'll be dead."

Don stopped walking. "You're joking, right?"

"No. I am not surviving this very well."

His eyes locked with mine and his face was serious. "You will. You are a lot stronger than you know."

I ignored his words of encouragement, he didn't know me well enough to make that statement with confidence. "Why are we going to the roof?" I asked.

"Blind luck."

"Huh?" I asked.

Don didn't answer.

I just followed, stopping every once in a while for breath. When we finally reached the top, I felt like I wanted to collapse.

He pushed open the roof door and I stepped out behind him. It was cold and the snow continued to trickle down. I saw the glow of a fire as he had cleared a walkway in the snow.

"This was a rooftop pool." Don pointed to the firepit. "Convenient, right?"

"Yes, and why...why are you lighting a fire on the roof?"

"We have no idea where Jane's father is. None. I thought if I lit that, in this darkness maybe they'll see us."

I inched back in surprise by what he said. How could he not be right? The rooftop seemed to be in the middle of nothing. I couldn't see anything out there. "That is really good thinking."

"Thank you."

"But do you really think he's out there? That he's alive?"

"I didn't at first. I do now."

"Why?"

He took hold of my arm and turned me around to go to the side of the roof behind the stairwell. The moonless sky along with the heavy clouds created a dark abyss on the one side of the hotel, but from where I stood there was a beacon of light...literally.

In the middle of the sea of black was an orange-tinted light emanating from the middle of a building in the distance. It was so bright in the darkness it illuminated a portion of the building.

Don's arm extended out to point at the source of the light. "I came up here and lit the fire in hopes of sending a signal. And I saw that instead. That building is big and tall. It has to be for a chopper of any size to land on the roof. I believe we may have found Jane's father," he said. "Mac, I'm pretty sure we found our way south."

TWENTY-ONE

READY

August 6

The look on his face was probably the same one I would produce. Gratefulness, relief, and love. They all appeared and cracked the typically ice exterior of Vice President Monroe Bates the moment he saw his daughter, Jane.

I suppose our group being mistaken as intruders didn't help. That was on Captain Holland. Him and his breaking into places.

Once daylight had arrived, we could see the building from the night before. It was farther away than we thought and the walk to it wasn't easy.

Snow had fallen overnight, adding a small but extra layer to what already was on the ground. But it was weak. It wasn't firm and icy like the road. Many times one of us would be walking and just drop in the snow.

It happened to everyone but Helen.

I would have expected Jane to never sink, seeing how she was so petite, but she dropped as fast as the rest of us. The tassel of her knit cap peeking through the show and the pink unicorn boo-boo bag stopping her from going too far down.

It was hard and slow-going. We had to stop several times and, by the time we arrived at what we believed was the location, we were literally frozen. Our wet clothes were stiff and hard.

Don was positive it was the right building and even if it wasn't the vice president, someone was inside.

When we finally arrived, I knew it had to be him in there. The building was that of a posh hotel. One of those that everyday, middle-class people couldn't afford.

Like every other building the snow was packed up against the entrance and Holland walked around until he found us a way in. He broke another window, climbed in, and set up a way for us to get inside.

We made our way into what looked like a greenhouse of sorts. Totally glass walls with tables and chairs set up to enjoy the shrubbery.

It wasn't long after we made it inside that we found ourselves facing four men with guns.

It was weird.

Everything in the world was falling apart, freezing over, yet these men were still dressed and clean; two in suits, two in military uniforms.

I believed we were done for and would get tossed out until Jane stepped forward and asked, "Is my father here?"

One of them recognized her and they lowered their weapons. Thank God. I was cold, my clothes were iced over, and my body shivered worse than when I had hypothermia.

They led us down a hall and to a stairwell. The walls were frosted over and I dreaded the prospect of walking up the stairs.

I didn't understand why they had to be six stories up. None of the men said anything or explained anything. We just walked behind them.

Despite everything looking iced over, the double doors to the room on the sixth floor looked fine.

I didn't look at the golden plaque next to the doors—at a glimpse it said suite. I figured it was big and probably had a fireplace, hence why they'd picked it.

One of the four men knocked once on the door and opened it.

The second the doors opened I felt the warmth.

Immediately I saw the source: a huge fireplace in the center of the room. Chairs and other items burned inside to make the fire roar.

Jane was behind us and stepped ahead. She dropped her bags, took off her knit cap, and called out, "Daddy?"

And that was when I saw it. The look on his face.

Monroe came from the other side of the fireplace and all color dropped from his face.

I had never seen a human being so overwhelmed, so happy and emotional. He raced to Jane, grabbing her.

"My God," he said. "I thought you were dead. I thought I lost you."

"You would have, Daddy, if it wasn't for my new friends."

She stepped back holding out her arm, showing us to him.

What a motley crew we must have appeared. Frozen over, haggard, tired, cold, and wet.

"Thank you," he said. "Please, all of you, come in. Get warm. I can't thank you enough."

He wasn't really focused on us, rightfully so. His words seemed more rehearsed and obligatory. He had his daughter back and that was what mattered to him at the moment.

Me, I was glad to see them reunited, but more happy to see that raging fire. I dropped my belongings, my hat and coat, and walked right over to the fire.

It was heaven, holding my frigid fingers in front of the flames.

I felt safe as if I could finally catch my breath. I also felt a little bit closer to finding my family. Monroe and Jane wouldn't be stuck in the building in the middle of Washington, D.C., they would get out, someway...I hoped. I also hoped they would take us with them. Any faster way south would work for me.

<><><><>

Almost as much as seeing his daughter, Monroe was happy to see a working radio. Although our signal didn't carry as far as he wished, he was able to get in touch with Richmond.

Once Holland handed over that radio it was as if he was unplugged. All his energy and power drained, the poor man just dropped in exhaustion to the floor, and curled up with a blanket and couch cushion as a pillow.

He didn't even eat.

Don was close to collapse as well. It was evident that he, too, finally felt at ease. He stayed close to the fire, eating from the MRE. He was laid back as it was, but now Don looked relaxed.

It was finally a moment to stop and relax. In those hours of reprieve I felt my lips starting to heal and my muscles aching less.

The suite we were in was huge. Several rooms with several fireplaces.

Me, Don, Helen, and Holland stayed in the main living area. After dinner, Jane went to bed.

Monroe stayed with us, talking. Perhaps he saw that Helen was more than ready to verbally pounce on him with questions.

Richmond, Virginia was the first of three relay points, he explained. With each destination being easier to travel to, since the weather wasn't as bad the farther south we went.

There were three destinations we would hit as we headed south by air. Each one a little farther from the previous one. It was the only way to do it flying by helicopter. A sort of relay.

"Is there a game plan?" Helen asked. "A final destination for you?"

Monroe nodded. "We will be meeting a boat in Miami and we will set course for Puerto Rico. We wanted South America, but we couldn't get permission to enter."

"Just you and your family?" she asked.

Monroe shook his head. "No, some members of congress are already there. Secretary of state, defense. I am eternally grateful to you for bringing my Jane to me. All of you are welcome to come with us."

I pursed my lips in an attempt to give a thankful smile. "We have to find our family."

"How many?" he asked.

"Three: my husband, two children."

"Four," Helen corrected. "Don't forget Fred."

I winced. "I'm sorry. Four. Fred is in Georgia."

"Four is not too many to bring along," said Monroe. "Don?" He looked at him. "What about you?"

"I'd like to help Mac with her quest first before I decide my fate," Don replied.

Monroe turned his attention to me. "How did you get separated?"

"A bridge washed out in Pennsylvania; Helen and I were on it. I've been asking at places we stopped if anyone had seen them. Some people told us they saw them with a man named Bob Abbot."

"Bob Abbot." Monroe said the name with familiarity.

"Oh, goodness," Helen said. "He must be a celebrity. You know him, too?"

Monroe chuckled. "Not from him being a celebrity. We overheard him on the radio. He said he was transporting people south. Was asking for stopping points. Fuel points." Monroe rubbed his chin. "I think a survival medical center in Fredrickson, Virginia offered him help. We won't be stopping far from there, maybe close enough to radio. But I would venture a guess once he hits there, it's smooth sailing south."

"No snow?" I asked.

"Oh, there's snow," he said. "But nothing like this. At least not yet. Maybe you'll have time after finding your family to join us."

"You're very kind," I said.

"No, you people are. I thought I'd lost my daughter."

"I know how that feels." My head lowered.

"So," Helen spoke up. "You want us to go on a ship filled with politicians, huh? That would prove interesting. Plus, when people find out you're abandoning our homeland for an island extension they may not be real happy."

"We need a solid place," Monroe said. "Sadly, the US is not solid. We need an establishing government for when this thing is over."

I glanced up, curious. "And that will be when?"

"Weather will calm in a month. That's what they tell me. The last of the big storms will be over. But…completely over, on a way back to normal?" Monroe shrugged. "I'm told five years."

"Five years!" Helen basted.

"Could be longer. It'll be decades before the north is truly habitable again."

"What happened?" I asked. "Do we know why this all occurred?"

"I could give you the science lingo, which I don't understand. In a nutshell, Artic shelf and polar vortex that was similar to the last ice age."

I leaned back. "Survival will be tough."

Monroe wrung his hands together. "I won't lie. It will be and the experts we talked to early on estimated that we could lose three quarters of the population when it's all said and done. Though, I am optimistic."

"When do you plan on leaving on this boat?" I asked.

"Within a day or two of getting there. Hopefully, we run into no problems when we leave. Last I heard another storm, the biggest one yet, is coming. It will blanket everything, even as far as Florida. Up here, we're not talking ten or twenty inches, we're talking feet."

"Oh shit," I gasped. "When?"

Monroe lifted his hands and shook his head. "We don't know. I lost communication, but we all need to hope it's after we get south. Because if we get caught in it, we will be stuck for weeks. And none of us," he said, "want that."

TWENTY-TWO

WHIP

August 6

We received word over the radio that the airlift would arrive in two hours. That gave us enough time to gather our things.

Even though we were being airlifted, Don didn't leave behind his homemade sled. He felt it important since we didn't know how much walking we would need to do in Georgia.

He folded it in half and loaded it back up the same way he did before we arrived in Washington.

I was more excited than nervous about flying in a helicopter. I kept thinking it was another day forward and another day closer to seeing my family again.

All of us made our way up the dark stairwell, six flights of stairs to get to the roof. It was colder than the day before, and that high up from the ground the wind whipped at us abrasively.

The expected storm hadn't come and, by the looks of the light gray sky, we still had time.

The surprise of the day to me was Helen. The usually stoic woman looked petrified—not even seeing how large the helicopter was eased her mind.

When it landed on the roof, Helen, Jane, and I were escorted inside while they loaded up.

It was semi-bench seating; the rows were across from each other inside, each with individual V-style belts over the head and chest.

"This isn't a good idea," Helen said, messing with her belt. "Look, they're strapping down our bags."

I glanced up. They were strapping in our belongings on a shelf above our heads. "In case of turbulence," I replied.

"Turbulence doesn't work right for helicopters," Helen said.

"You may be right," Jane said. "This doesn't feel right."

"Please don't encourage her fear," I told Jane.

"No," Helen argued. "She is right. She has that psychic sense about her."

"No, she doesn't," I said. "We'll be fine."

"Strap in," Don said as he took a seat next to me.

"I did."

He reached over, checked my straps like an amusement park attendant and tightened it. He then got up and fixed Helen's. "We'll be fine, Helen," he told her. "These are experienced pilots."

"Yeah, well, even an experienced driver has hell to pay on ice," Helen said. "One good wind and we're tail spinning to our deaths."

My immediate reaction was to scoff about it, then something clicked and I thought if Helen was worried, perhaps I should be too.

I was ready to help her, to share her worries until she went overboard. At least I thought so.

"Young man," she called out to the pilot as he checked everything. "Young man. Can I have a helmet?"

"Ma'am."

"A helmet. Please."

He didn't question any further, he just went to the front of the plane and returned with one.

"Thank you," Helen took the straps on it to secure it. "And a life jacket."

"Ma'am, we're not going over water."

"You don't think?" Helen asked. "What is snow?"

"Yes, ma'am." Again he headed to the front of the chopper.

"Make it two."

I refrained from saying, *Really, Helen?* and let it go.

He brought back two foam vest jackets. She undid her buckle long enough to put on one vest and tie the other to her hips because, as she said, they'd be the first to break in a crash.

"Let it go," Don said. "If they help, it's a good thing."

I supposed they were her security blanket.

If she needed those things who was I to question? But I ended up going from pacifying to fearful, especially as we lifted off and the pilot warned it could be a rough ride. When he said that, I envied Helen, no matter how ridiculous she looked.

Helicopters, especially ones as big as the one we used, were not conducive to conversation. At least not to those of us without an earpiece. I wanted to talk to Don or Helen, but unless we shouted, I wouldn't hear them if they did speak to me. We had resorted to glances of assurance in the moments after liftoff. That was all we could do.

Once I was accustomed to the noise, I could hear bits and pieces. A few voices here and there.

The first real bump of rough air came about twenty minutes into our journey. I didn't think too much of it, until it happened again.

The helicopter bounced and swayed. I looked over to see Helen holding onto her belt by her shoulders. Her eyes were closed and lips moving.

The helicopter moved in a weird way; it was as if it was being carried instead of flown. Lifted along by the wind was my only guess.

Monroe and Holland were across from us, both were wearing headsets. Monroe held on to his and I could tell he was listening to the pilot talk.

"No," he spoke loudly. "Don't chance it. Radio if you can, let me know what we're doing. Keep an eye out."

"What's going on?" Don shouted.

"Some sort of windstorm!" Monroe replied. "We're about twenty miles out from Fredrickson!"

Then his voice trailed off in the noise as the chopper swayed more.

"We're landing?" Don asked.

"As best as we can!" Monroe shouted. "Hold tight."

The chopper was going to set down. I was okay with that. I guess the pilot just had to find a place to do so, but he was up against some steep odds.

It was worse than any turbulence I'd ever experienced. It was more like an amusement park ride. Why not? We were strapped in like one.

We went left to right, up and down, jolting every few seconds. It wasn't flying, I could feel that the pilot was fighting whatever force was controlling us.

I refrained from screaming, or even panicking, but I kept thinking how right Helen was. It was hard not to be scared when in a situation so far out of our control.

The chopper lifted up quickly, and almost as if it was hit with a huge baseball bat, flew backwards and snapped hard in a roll to its side. When it did, something above us holding our belongings must have snapped. A black backpack flew down, fast and furiously, slamming into Holland.

It hit him hard in the face. He didn't see it coming or knew what hit him. The pack bounced off him and onto the floor. His head slumped forward and all I saw was blood all over him.

Don didn't hesitate. He immediately took off his belt and leaped toward Holland.

I wanted to shout at him. Yell at him to get strapped back in, but there was no time.

Just when he grabbed onto Holland the chopper started spinning out of control. Like a needle on a compass trying to find direction, we went into a tailspin. It wasn't a smooth one. We spun around, dropping and bouncing. My eyes couldn't focus, everything moved around me. Like Helen, I grabbed hold of my belt and closed my eyes.

There is a profound calm that proceeds a moment when you know you're going to die. In that chopper, at that very moment, I knew we were done. I accepted it. We were going to crash.

I would never see my children again, they would never know I survived that bridge.

I prepared for impact, bracing myself.

The pilot tried, he really tried, but the force of nature was far too much. The chopper spun until it slammed into the ground. The belt over my shoulders cut into me as the restraining device fought against the force to keep me in place.

We didn't stop when we hit the ground with a slam and a loud crack. The body of the chopper rolled several times, then spun like a top until it came to a stop.

During it all my body went from side to side, jolted up and down.

When we finally slowed down, I thought, *This is it, we are going to explode.*

But we didn't.

In the seconds after the crash, I could hear the whirl of the blade as it struggled in its last spins.

When I realized we weren't exploding, I opened my eyes. We'd survived. How did we survive?

Still belted in the seat, every part of my body ached and I could feel the frigid air blasting at me. I immediately looked to my right. Helen was still buckled in.

"Helen," I called. "Are you okay?"

"Fine. Fine. You?"

I nodded and looked to my left. "Jane?"

She was struggling to unbuckle her belt. "I'm fine. We need to move. We need to go now. Daddy?"

Nothing.

Then a second later, almost panicked, Jane freed herself from her harness and jumped from her seat. "Oh my God," she called out.

I looked forward to where Monroe, Holland, and the two security soldiers had been seated.

Nothing was there.

The chopper had become a wreckage and half the craft was missing. Gone. We'd been thrown or had they? I didn't know.

What I did know was that I couldn't see anyone else that had been on that chopper.

They were gone.

Like Jane, I hurriedly undid my belt, jumped from my seat and bolted forward.

As I jumped from the wreckage, I saw we had crash-landed in some sort of wooded area. Snow was everywhere. I saw a chopper door, a backpack, tree limbs, and what looked like a piece of a blade.

But I didn't see anyone.

Where were they?

TWENTY-THREE

TRUDGE

"Jane! Janey, where are you?" the distant voice carried to us, fighting to be heard over the increasingly howling wind.

Jane turned to her left and right, then chased after the voice.

I spun to the remaining portion of the helicopter. "Stay in here," I told Helen. "Away from the elements."

Helen came from the cockpit area. "Pilot's alive. I'm gonna help him."

I nodded. "Someone is calling out. I think it's Monroe. Maybe...maybe Don is with him."

I was a few seconds into my run, following Jane's footprints, when the snow started to fall. Big flakes slowly falling like on Christmas morning. Jane and her pink coat stood out making her easy to spot and follow.

As we made it through the snow, we had to move slowly. Running wasn't an option. Jane disappeared over a crest and when I arrived I saw her embracing Monroe.

Around them, scattered about, was a trail of belongings. Backpacks, duffel bags, and Jane's unicorn boo-boo bag stuck out like a sore thumb.

Her hand reached up to his forehead. I couldn't hear what they were saying, even as I moved close.

I watched Monroe point and I saw the rest of the helicopter, the portion we lost.

There was no hesitation, I hurried that way, my heart beating fast in my chest. The smell of oil was strong and it carried as I walked into the wind on my way to that portion of the helicopter. It was hard to tell when I'd gotten out of my seat how much was actually missing of the chopper. All I'd seen was the outside. But down the embankment was just a small section of the chopper.

I was behind Jane and Monroe as they walked around the section of metal.

My face instantly felt flush then hot when I saw the only person there was Holland. He was strapped to the seat. He moved his head back and forth.

"Hey," Jane said to him. "Can you hear me?"

Holland nodded.

"Can you walk? Do you think you can walk?" she asked.

"I don't know."

Jane looked at her father. "Maybe we should find Don's sled."

"No," I said. "We should find Don."

I backed up, rushing from the wreckage. Where was Don? Where were the other two soldiers?

"Don!" I screamed out. I was uncertain he'd hear me at all, especially with the wind gusting so loud. But we heard Monroe when he called.

"Don!"

I felt so desperate.

The luggage and bags were there. I walked a little beyond the wreckage. Through the snow about fifty feet away I saw something gray.

I raced that way, my feet sliding as I tried to keep my footing in the accumulated snow.

When I arrived, I saw it was a section of the bench seat. Snow had started to build up on it and it tilted forward with the back facing me.

If there was anyone strapped in, they were face down in the snow.

I looked.

There they were.

It was the two missing soldiers.

I didn't know if they were alive or dead, but I had to check.

The 'L' shape of the seat was like a tent, creating a small pocket that I could reach under and check.

I was so happy to see neither of the soldiers were buried, or drowning in the snow, but I did see blood. A lot of it.

For the last several days I had been wearing two pairs of gloves. My knit ones, then a larger pair over them with a plastic bag in between. I had taken off the first layer and the bag on the chopper.

My fingertips were exposed and my hands were cold.

I reached and touched the first soldier, trying to feel for a pulse. The blood was like cake icing glazing his neck. I couldn't feel anything. It was hard to tell if his flesh was really cold and hard or if it was my fingers. I wasn't a medical professional and while Jane claimed to be, I was certain she wasn't one either.

I made my way to the other side of to check the second soldier. He was the same. I didn't even look, and as horrible as it was, I couldn't wait around to assess them. I had to find Don.

But I wasn't thinking. I wasn't registering I had also just been in and survived a major accident. It didn't register that parts of my body were hurt, and a reasonable thought process was lacking in my brain.

I would take a few steps, call out his name, look left and right, then repeat.

The wind whipped the light snow about making things worse.

Then it finally hit me. Monroe and Holland were over the crest some hundred yards or so from where I was, and Don hadn't been in his seat when we crashed, so it would make sense that he was somewhere in between.

I held on to the hope that there was so much snow he had to be alright from any impact.

As far as length of time went, I hadn't known him long, but he was no less a friend than someone I had known all my life.

Calling out his name over and over, occasionally losing my breath when a gust of wind blasted me, I moved hastily back toward the wreckage.

"Don!"

"Mac."

I stopped moving.

"Mac! Come quick!" It was Helen's voice.

It was possible the weather had my ears playing tricks on me, but I swore she sounded closer.

How could that be? I told her to stay back with the pilot.

Sure enough, just as I got close to our section of the chopper, a quick look to my left and I saw Helen.

Why was she out?

I moved her way. I didn't have time for nonsense, we needed to find Don.

"Helen," I rushed to her. "I can't…"

"Mac." She grabbed my arms. "The pilot said to look here, close. As soon as I came out I saw…"

My eyes shifted to beyond her. "Pink snow," I said with a whisper.

It wasn't the first time I had seen it, and I wasn't being fooled into believing it was some sort of algae.

The snow had fallen just enough that when it landed, it created a veil of sorts, making the blood look pink.

I brushed by Helen and followed what would be a trail. The first patch of blood was about the size of a baseball, then a steady trail in a zigzag manner. He had wandered, probably confused.

I saw the snow-covered mound a few feet ahead and knew it had to be Don.

"Oh my God." I ran over.

He was on his side, his back facing me. I dropped down in front of him, my knees sinking into the snow. There was some blood surrounding him, thankfully not a lot.

"Don."

He coughed.

I wheezed out a heavy breath of gratefulness and Don, with a soft groan, rolled to his back.

"Mac," he said with a struggle. His face winced just a little as if he were trying to hide the pain.

There was no hiding what caused it.

When my eyes cased down, I saw a hammer-sized metal object protruding from his gut just under the rib cage.

"Hold on," I said, rushed. "Hold on." I looked over my shoulder. "Help! Helen, get help."

I didn't know what to do, I really didn't. Short of what I had learned in basic first aid, which was not to pull out the object, I was lost.

"Don," I whimpered his name. "I don't know what to do."

"You…" He coughed. "Can't do anything. Go."

"I can't leave."

"You have to."

I heard the light thump near me and looked over to see that pink unicorn boo-boo bag.

"No one's going anywhere," Jane said calmly and reached for her bag. "Excuse me, Mac, I need to get in here."

Was she serious? I saw the look of horror on Don's face. Maybe that's what it was. I wanted to snap at her, make a comment that now wasn't the time to play three times, flunked-out nurse.

Then she unzipped the unicorn bag. It opened wide like a book and inside was a well-stocked, organized medical kit. Some of the items had children's stickers on them.

She took hold of Don's wrist for a few seconds. "Your pulse is good, Don. I like to see that." She reached down and gently palpitated near his impalement. "It doesn't feel real, real deep to me. But I can't take a chance and pull it out. You know that, Don. We need to get to shelter and I'll help you then. We can do this. Fredrickson is no more than fifteen miles. Last I heard we walked that much before." She looked over her shoulder to me. "We need to move fast. I need you to find his sled for me. Okay. Get it here stat. I need everyone ready to move."

I nodded and stood.

She reached back into her pack, pulling out two small, paper-wrapped items. She opened them both exposing syringes. "Are you allergic to penicillin?" she asked him.

195

Don shook his head.

She grabbed a vial, and with steady hands inserted the syringe into the vial. "I'm going to give you a shot of penicillin, then something to ease the pain and keep you calm. It's going to be a rough journey. You ready?"

I backed up watching as she administered the medicine. I now remembered where I had seen the sled and headed to find it.

A part of me was in shock, not only because of the crash and Don, but because Jane snapped into action, shaming the cynical side of me that based a judgement on her privileged demeanor and pink unicorn boo-boo bag.

I was wrong.

I'm glad I was.

It wasn't going to be easy for any of us. Especially Don.

If we'd thought the walk to D.C. was bad, it was nothing compared to what we were facing now. We weren't sure exactly how far away we were. The pilot estimated ten miles. But we had to hope for some sort of shelter so we could stop every so often to give Don a break.

It wasn't the ideal way to do things, but it was the only logical way.

Holland could walk, but it was automated and, mentally, he seemed more out of it than Don. The pilot had a head injury. He and Monroe each placed an arm over Holland and nearly carried him.

Jane, Helen, and I carried Don.

Strapped to the sled, we each pulled a rope, with Jane stopping and bracing his wound if we went over a rough area.

We didn't want to leave any of our bags—some of them were our only source of warmth and food. We took only what we truly needed. We moved slowly. Any quick pace was impossible.

No sooner had we started our journey than the mega storm began. Or at last the start of it.

The afternoon sky darkened to an early evening gray and the snow fell at an astronomical rate, thick and heavy. The wind made it blustery and hard to see our feet in front of us

The best laid plans...

There was never a safe place to stop. We had Don covered with a blanket and had to continuously pause to clear it of snow. Not a single part of my body, Helen's, or anyone else's wasn't frozen over, covered like a snowman from head to toe.

I believed the ten miles was a thousand. A trip we wouldn't make.

There was no way to calculate how far we had walked. The storm inhibited us from seeing what was ahead. Frederickson could have been right there and we wouldn't have known.

All of us had reached the point our legs were like rubber, buckling without warning.

My shoulder hurt from the rope and the weight.

"What is that?" Jane yelled.

I hadn't a clue what she was talking about, then I saw. Round lights danced in the distance. There were six of them that I could make out. They moved in no particular direction.

Their presence caused us to stop. It seemed like a gift to Helen to not have to move. Her head dropped forward and I could see her shoulders bouncing up and down. She was worn out, how could she not be. I was younger and I felt as if I wanted to drop. I could only imagine how she felt.

A hand came down on my shoulder, drawing my attention away from Helen. Through the corner of my eye I saw the pilot staggering right before us and stopping.

What was he doing? Then I watched him lift his arm, aim slightly high, and fire.

It wasn't a normal gun, it was a flare gun and he shot it at a tree. It hit hard exploding outward. The blazing red flare not only lit up the area blinded by snow, but it started a small fire. Like Helen, he lowered his head in relief. We were all illuminated and I could feel the heat. I just wanted to get closer.

The lights moved and headed our way. The pilot knew exactly what they were.

Soon, I did too when three snowmobiles arrived.

Nearly on the verge of tears, afraid to shed any liquid from my eyes, I whimpered. Don would be okay. At least I hoped he would.

The snowmobiles were the type seen in movies, they each had two seats and one of them had a sled that I imagined was for somebody injured.

Three men in heavy parkas striped with bright yellow reflective tape walked over to us. It was hard to see their faces, they were so covered.

"We'll take him!" one told me. "Put him down gently."

I released my rope and he took hold of the sled. He and another man carried Don. I followed, watching as they loaded him onto a medical sled, strapping him in.

"Hey," I said to Don. "We're gonna be okay."

Ever so slightly Don nodded as he pressed his lips together in a closed-mouth smile.

Jane drew the attention of the two men as they finished up with Don. "We have two injured." She pointed to Holland and the pilot. "They need medical attention as well."

"Our orders," a third man spoke from behind us, "are to retrieve the vice president first and foremost. We can take those two men, the vice president, and then return for you." He signaled to the two rescue workers to get Holland and the pilot. "Put them in."

"Right away, Chief," one replied.

They immediately strapped Holland and the pilot in the snow-mobiles, and they didn't wait to take off.

I looked once more at Don on that sled, moving from view and from the light of the flare. I turned and walked back to Helen and Monroe. "They'll be back," I said. "They need to take you." I looked at Monroe. "They'll come back for us."

"We need to move, Mr. Vice President," the chief said.

"Don't be absurd," Monroe replied. "Take this woman." He indicated to Helen. "She's been walking and was in a helicopter crash. She's seventy-four years old."

"And fit as a fiddle, you asshole," Helen told him. "I'm fine."

"No," Monroe argued. "You're worn out."

"We're all worn out," she blasted him. "You were on the bad side of the chopper. You go."

"Sir," the chief said. "We are to retrieve you first. We'll be back. It won't take long. I have orders."

"Then I can stay. Those are my orders."

"Oh," Helen scoffed. "Like the vice president has any authority."

"Excuse me!" the chief yelled. "One of you in the snowmobile now! This storm is not going to wait."

"Helen," I said. "Please. I'd feel better if you went and made sure they took care of Don. Please. Besides, we're going to Fredrickson. You may find out about the kids. Bob Abbot was there."

"Then I'll go. I'll ask around so when you arrive, I'll know something." She turned to the chief. "I'll go."

The chief reached for her arm. Helen stopped and slid her backpack from her shoulder. She reached in the front zipper compartment and pulled out a bottle. "Here." She handed it to me. "It will keep you warm." When I took it, she placed her hands over mine. "I'd give you my gloves," she said. "But I took them off in the chopper."

"Me too."

"Oh!"

"Ma'am," the chief called.

"One second," Helen snapped. She pulled her hood from her head and undid her plastic bonnet she still wore underneath. She handed it to me. "You took yours off on the chopper. Wear this. I want it back."

"Absolutely."

She reached up and tapped me on the cheek, smiled at Monroe, then Jane. "Good job, girly, on Don." Then she grabbed the Chief's arm. "I'm ready."

His snowmobile wasn't far. He secured her, then came back to us.

"I should be no longer than an hour. Stay close to the fire from the flare." He handed Monroe an orange gun. "Should it die down, hit it again. We'll return as soon as possible."

"Thank you," Monroe said.

The chief gave a nod, returned to the snowmobile and within seconds he had left.

I watched the taillights as they disappeared into the snow.

"Let's get close to the fire," Jane suggested.

I cradled the pint-size bottle of booze and glanced at Monroe. "Thank you. Thank you for sending her."

"She looked tired. To be honest, I don't know how she did it."

"She's one tough woman," Jane said. "That's for sure."

"Don't I know it," I replied.

With all that was going on, so focused on the arrival of the snow-mobiles, the relief of them taking our injured, and the events unfolding round us, the storm, as strange as it was, had faded into the background of my attention.

It wasn't for very long.

Once we were alone, left behind, it was evident again how bad things were and how bad they would get.

The snow had fallen to my knees and still kept coming.

While we were trudging through the beginning of the storm carrying Don, I had believed it would be the death of us all. I feared that storm. Not for the unknown quality of it, but because I was in it and knew it would only get worse.

I stood with Monroe and Jane in the orange glow, catching the heat when the chill of the wind didn't overwhelm it. Sharing my bottle with them and watching the whirlwind around us, I feared the storm a little less.

We wouldn't be in it for long. Even though it didn't seem like it at that very moment, we had indeed been rescued. Something I'd never seen happening.

TWENTY-FOUR

SNOW BALLED

It was scary and dark when we arrived at the eight-story hospital and it was only four o'clock.

The first floor was completely buried in snow and we entered the second story through a window which had been previously broken for access.

We were dropped off and helped inside. Afterwards, the snow-mobiles took off and they lowered a tarp over the windows to block out the storm.

It was the first time all day I felt the silence.

There was a woman there who introduced herself as Donna as she shook hands with Monroe.

"Where are the snowmobiles going?" Monroe asked. "They just dropped us off."

"The parking garage in hopes they don't get buried in there," she replied. "The snow is supposed to get pretty high."

"Our people?" Jane asked. "They came the first round."

"I didn't see them," she answered. "They were taken to the other side of the building to the east wing. Even though this is a hospital, we handle the main medical there. I know the one man is in surgery."

"Can we see them?" I asked.

"As soon as they're treated, they'll join you," she said. "We're happy to have you."

"I'm a nurse," Jane said. "Do you need my help?"

"Not right now, but it looks like she does." Donna glanced at me.

I suppose she meant my lips.

"I can get you some supplies," Donna said to Jane.

"No." Jane shook her head and held up her bag. "I should have it in here, if not then I'll ask."

"Great," Donna said. "Come on in. We try to keep people together for warmth and away from the windows. I'll get you situated and see if I can get you some food. It won't be much—we are rationing because we don't know how long we'll be here."

I felt bad. The last thing I wanted was for them to give us their food, but I didn't know if we had even brought any in our bags. Helen had taken her bag with her. She had food. She was probably sitting right next to Don, occasionally sipping from another stashed bottle.

We followed Donna as she took us upstairs two floors. It looked like a doctor's office or a place where conferences were held. She told us the main room, a communications room, was there. Monroe went to the radio to try to get information on the storm. Jane and I went into another room that looked more like a waiting area. People each had their individual space, but there were a lot of survivors there. Lit by candles, everyone sat on blankets or in the chairs staring at us when we walked in.

Jane and I took a corner, and she immediately opened up her boo-boo bag. I huffed in a soft chuckle, running my hand over it.

"What?" Jane asked.

"I didn't take you seriously before because you called it a boo-boo bag."

"That's because I'm focused on pediatrics," she said. "And why would you take me seriously? I failed my boards three times." She opened a packet and pulled out a small gauze. She dampened it with saline and gently began cleaning my lips. "I kept thinking maybe if I had gone to a different school I would have passed."

I winced in pain. "How do you think Don is?"

"Hard to say. The object didn't seem too deep, but then again, he wasn't reacting to the pain."

"Is that bad?"

"It could be. I'm sure he's in good hands. Then again, he isn't moving or going anywhere just yet."

"I don't think any of us are."

"No," she said. She reached back into the bag. "I'm putting some ointment on these lips."

"They're that bad?"

"Yeah. You're not going to be kissing anyone any time soon."

I chuckled. "I'm sure Glen will say he's not kissing them either."

She smiled gently with a *hmm* and leaned back. "Done. Anything else hurt? Are you sore?"

"A little. But I'm fine."

She handed me a bottle of water and two pills. "Ibuprofen. Take them."

It was easier said than done. I had to place the pills in my mouth and drink the water without letting my lips touch the rim. But I managed. "Thank you."

"You're welcome."

"I mean…thank you. I never told you that before," I said

"You just did."

"No. I mean for the bridge and what happened at the overpass. You saved our lives and we never said anything."

"I didn't look at it that way."

"How did you know?" I asked. "It was extremely intuitive."

"I have a gift, I like to say. I just wish my gift would work when taking the boards." She laughed and put her things back in the bag. "I can't always control them. Never have been able to. I just knew, even with all the rides I was offered, I wasn't supposed to take them."

"I thought you said you missed your ride?"

"One or two I did, the rest I opted against. Until I met Don."

"Can you tap into that intuition? Will he be okay?"

"I think so. Now…you relax. I'm going to find my father and check on him."

I gave her a smile, though not too broad—it hurt to move my lips. Jane stood, holding her boo-boo bag, stepping over people, and making her way out.

It felt strange in that room. I knew it wasn't late, it was probably the reason everyone was awake. They fed me a small bowl of potatoes which I consumed hungrily and with guilt.

Was I taking from them? Did they have the food to spare? I was grateful that I had a roof over my head and the room was warm.

So many people, they all looked upon me as if I were an anomaly. Their faces crying out an expression of some sort of shock.

We all were in shock. One way or another. Either through the events that had brought us together or facing our world which was falling apart.

It had been hours and we still hadn't heard anything yet about Don. Jane came to tell us Holland had to get multiple sutures on his face, the pilot had a concussion, and both were resting.

She implied the surgery for Don was probably more complicated than expected and was why it was taking longer.

We just had to wait.

I did. With my issued blanket, the trying day and exhaustion had kicked in. I dozed off curled up on a green vinyl chair.

I woke with a jolt. A feeling of confusion followed by anger for falling asleep overwhelmed me.

The room was quiet except for an occasional cough. It had to be late, it was even darker than before.

I felt bad for abandoning Helen like that—while I slept and ate, she sat diligently in a hallway somewhere, holding post and waiting on news of Don. I decided it had been long enough and I would seek them out.

At the very least I would relieve Helen of waiting duty.

I felt the stiffness of my muscles when I stood, the ache from the crash and walking.

After I left the room, my goal was to find Donna and have her help me make it to the medical region.

But I didn't find her. It was like looking for a needle in a haystack. Every room I peeked into had so many people.

She had probably sought a quiet place to rest.

I had the unshakable feeling of being in a nightmare, questioning if I were asleep or awake. I couldn't find anyone I knew.

Monroe and Jane more than likely had the best accommodations, that was probably why I didn't locate them.

To be truthful my search wasn't for them, it was for the medical wing.

Finally, I found someone who armed me with a flashlight and directed me where to go. It seemed easy enough and I wasn't as far away as I had thought. A couple turns then through the double doors, down a hall and another set of double doors would bring me to where they treated people.

Once I found and stepped through that first set of double doors, it was a different world.

The acoustics were different, the temperature was much colder

A long hallway lined with windows connected the wings.

The windows were useless, I couldn't see anything outside. But I could hear it. The storm was relentless; the wind howled in a deep demonic way, while the snow fell so hard. I could hear it battering the building.

I saw a light through the small rectangular windows on the double doors at the other end of the hall.

When I walked through, it had a typical hospital floor feel. A medicine cart was halfway up. I spotted a nurses' station down the way with a lantern on the counter.

Open doors to patient rooms were on both sides of the hall. A female nurse or medical professional paced back and forth looking at an open folder. I figured I'd peek in each room as I passed. Maybe find Holland, the pilot, and Don. Surely, Don was done with surgery and in a room somewhere.

I had made it to all of three rooms when the nurse startled me by asking in a whisper, "Hi, can I help you?"

Nearly screaming, I caught myself, cusped my hand over my mouth and shook my head. "Sorry."

"It's okay. Sorry to scare you," she said.

I saw the name tag; I believe it said Amber. "I was looking for my friends. Two of them I heard were fine. One with facial stitches…"

"Oh, the helicopter crash," she said. "With the vice president."

"That's us."

She nodded.

"It's been a while, I mean like hours. I haven't heard anything. I just need an update."

"Someone should have found you," she said as she folded her arms. "I'm…I'm so sorry. The other person…I'm sorry."

At first I thought she was apologizing for not giving me an update, then it hit me. I felt all the air escape from my lungs as the blood seemed to drain from my head and form a knot in my gut. I swallowed a hard lump in my throat. "Sorry as in…dead."

Wearing a sympathetic look, she nodded. "Yes, I am very sorry."

"Oh my God." My hand shot to my mouth. "Oh my God." Poor Don. I felt horrible for him and all he had been through.

"We did everything we could," she said.

"I know. I just thought…"

"We tried. We really did. But there were injuries that weren't visible externally. Then exposure to the elements for so long didn't help. All combined they were very hard odds to beat."

"Thank you."

"We don't think there was much pain." She reached out and placed her hand on my shoulder.

I didn't know how to feel. Hurt, shock, sadness. I lowered my head.

"If it helps, she went fast."

My eyes widened and my head lifted. That word, that single word felt like an electric knife into my chest.

She?

My legs weakened.

"She's in the last room on the right, if you want…"

I didn't even wait for her to finish. Wobbly legs and all, I took off running.

Please, no. Please. I prayed and pleaded with each pounding footstep and each racing beat of my heart.

The hallway wasn't long enough for all the prayers I needed to say. I was winded and dizzy from emotions when I stepped into the room.

It was dark, but my flashlight showed me enough.

I wanted to die, just collapse and forget everything.

I wished to God I had some of that intuition Jane had, because it was another thing I never saw coming.

There was a single examining table in the room and a sheet covered her body from the waist down. It was hard to really see her. I couldn't tell if she looked peaceful or scared, but I could tell one thing for absolutely certain.

It was Helen. She…was gone.

TWENTY-FIVE

DRIFT

August 7

She never once left my side when both my children were born. Not for a sandwich or a breath of fresh air. Every pain, every breath, every push. She took care of my family when I couldn't. When there were times I swore she hated me, never did I doubt that Helen loved me.

Despite it all she was there for me, and when it counted, I wasn't there for her.

It broke my heart she was gone. I wasn't there and she died alone. Helen of all people would have never left anyone by themselves.

She was that person who visited every sick friend in the hospital, she was company for anyone who needed it.

They needed to move her to the cold room, a place where they kept the bodies of those who'd passed. Nurse Amber told me they lost a lot of people due to element exposure.

But I couldn't leave her side. I kept asking for more time, even as the sky slightly lightened with the morning. I sat by the table, my hand on hers, her book bag on my lap.

By what I guessed was first thing in the morning, news had spread, at least to our crew.

Jane was the first to come. I heard the patter or her running feet just before she entered the room with a loud, shocking gasp.

"Oh, Mac. Oh, Mac, I'm sorry." Jane inched into the room. "I just found out."

"No one told me. I discovered by accident when I came to check on Don."

"I heard he's doing well."

I nodded, my fingers rubbing against Helen's hand. "I'd like to be the one to tell him. He doesn't know. What happened, Jane? How did this happen?"

"They told me she just collapsed, they tried to revive her, but she was gone. It happened that fast."

"Do you think your dad has that intuition? I mean he insisted she go."

Jane shook her head. "My dad just has a good heart. I didn't feel it. I didn't...I didn't even see it with her."

"None of us did. I never would have thought this would happen. I expected her to outlive me."

"I did, too."

Quickly, I looked up to her.

"I'm being honest. I thought she'd outlive me. I remember thinking when we were carrying Don, we're all gonna fall over and Helen will be the last one standing."

"Was that it?" I asked. "You think we strained her too much?"

"No. It didn't help, I'll be honest, but Amber told me she had internal injuries. We don't know what happened to her during the crash."

"And she was tough," I said. "She only complained about being cold, until, well, it was cold."

Jane walked around to face me and gently spoke. "They need to take her, Mac. Go see Don. She wouldn't want you sitting here with her body."

"You're right." Slowly, I stood. My muscles ached and were still sore. I leaned over Helen, placing my mouth near her ear. "Thank you for everything you have done for me and our family. I will tell them how hard you tried to get to them. You'll be with me always." I brought my lips to her forehead. It was painful, not my lips, but touching her firm and cold skin.

The night before Jane had jokingly told me I wouldn't be kissing anyone anytime soon. I didn't doubt that, I just never would have thought the kiss I did deliver, would be a last kiss to Helen.

<><><><>

"I'm sorry for your loss," Monroe said to me the second I stepped from Helen's holding room and into the hall. He had been waiting out there. He looked refreshed and shaved, which struck me as odd. Perhaps because he wanted to be a symbol of leadership. "I didn't expect this and I didn't know until Jane told me."

"I know, no one did."

"These people running this place, they are doing this as volunteers not as some government. I can't explain why they didn't tell you."

I shook my head. "They're busy. I'm grateful for their help."

"Have you seen Don?" he asked.

"Not yet. I'm on my way there now."

"Give him my best and tell him I will stop by. I'll also have Jane pop in and visit him as well."

"Thank you."

"And make sure he knows to take his time. Get well. We're not going anywhere. None of us are. Not yet."

"Will we?" I asked.

"I'm sure of it. If not, we'll think of something."

We would. I excused myself again to go to Don. Another thing to feel bad about, not seeing him sooner.

I had asked about Don, I didn't forget him, I just hadn't been to see him. When Amber would come in to see if I needed anything, I'd ask. She told me Don's surgery went well, the metal wasn't as deep as it had looked and had missed anything vital.

The storm was still beating down on us. I had forgotten what it was like to see the sun or the blue of the sky, it had been so long. The dismal day added more sadness to my mourning. Shrouding any light from hitting me. I drowned in guilt over losing Helen. She didn't deserve to die alone in a cold hospital room. I should have been there.

After leaving Monroe, I made my way to Don's room, knocking once before heading in. The back of his bed was up some and he was awake.

"Hey," I said.

"Hey. You're okay," Don replied.

"I know I didn't come. No one told me anything or I would have come to check on you."

"It's okay."

"How are you feeling?" I asked.

"I don't feel too bad. They say I need to rest for a while. I'm stuck here, but I'll fight it if you want to leave."

"Don, we're all stuck here," I said.

"How much snow?'

"Honestly? I haven't even looked out."

213

"Your lips look better."

I tried not to smile or frown, it hurt too much. "Jane put something on it. Who would have known she was really good at what she does?"

"Helen did," Don said with almost a hint of sadness. "She said to me the other night that she would bet any money Jane was a good nurse. How could she not be when she went to nursing school three times."

"Don, listen…"

"I'm sorry, Mac. I am."

"For?" I asked, slightly confused.

"For your loss of Helen. I am sorry."

"I didn't know you knew."

"How could I not?" he asked. "She was right here."

I inhaled sharply. "She what?"

"No one told you?"

"No one even told me she died. I found out when I was trying to get an update about you. She was here with you when it happened?"

I brought my trembling fingers to my mouth. Hearing that made me so happy. "She wasn't alone?"

"No." Don shook his head. "Not before or during."

"You don't know how relieved I am to hear that. I was so upset thinking she died alone." I grabbed a chair and pulled it to his bedside and sat down. "Tell me about the last moments, please.

"She was right where you were. Sitting in the chair. When I came to, she was across the room and she moved closer."

"Did she look bad to you? Sick?"

"It's hard to say. We had a bad day, all of us."

I nodded.

"Anyhow, she told me to rest, she was staying with me and they were going to get you and Jane."

"So the operation didn't take long," I said.

"No. I tried to rest but eventually I woke all the way up and we talked."

"About? What did you talk about?"

"The kids. Glen. You. How she'd found Cleo's boot on the chopper and put it in her bag," he said. "Because she knew you wouldn't be able to sleep without it. She joked, you know, about how it was one more thing she survived."

"Years of being a crossing guard."

"That's what she said," Don told me. "We talked a while. So many things. I'm sure they'll all come back to me. We laughed. We worried a little because we hadn't heard from you. She kept taking drinks from a bottle in her bag. She…then said, 'Oh, Don, I think I am having empathy pains. My belly hurts.' Then she looked at me and fell forward to my bed. She was in that chair and her head landed by my arm. I called for help. They came. But she was gone, Mac. She went that fast. She didn't know."

Slowly, I exhaled. I hated that I had lost Helen, but I was so relieved she went quickly, smiling and not alone. She had come so far and I knew it would devastate Glen to hear she survived the washout of the bridge but not the journey to find them.

It would be a while until I found them. But I would.

For her sake, I had to keep going, I had to find our family. I needed them in my life and they needed to know that Helen fought and forged forward to be with them, despite the odds.

TWENTY-SIX

CALM

August 30

For four days straight the storm was relentless, pounding us with alternating rounds of snow and ice. When it had finished and everything calmed, we were buried in twenty-five feet. The sky was still clouded over, creating a frozen tundra that used to be a city.

We needed something to make the time pass. Even though the storm was over, we couldn't leave. The snow was too deep and the temperatures too deadly. Plus, it took a week to finally reach anyone by radio to set up an evacuation.

The rescue would come, we just had to wait.

The storm had hit everywhere. The south, not hit as badly as we were, would warm up some. That's what we waited on. The north…it would be a long time before it was ever green, maybe even longer than my lifetime. I couldn't imagine with all the snow how truly long it would take to go away. Before it all, when we had a big snow, it didn't matter how warm it was, it took forever for the snow-plowed mounds in the supermarket parking lot to go away.

The children found a twisted amusement looking out the windows at the snow, then turning away and walking with sun blindness into their friends.

I watched them a lot. They made me think of my own children, how they were always resourceful in entertaining themselves.

The children were the saddest part of it all. So many of them without parents or a family to help them. They were reliant on strangers for survival and love. I just hoped as strangers we could relinquish our selfishness and bitterness over our losses and find a way to help them.

My time was spent dealing with the loss of Helen and missing my family. Each passing day it grew harder to wait and my patience ran thin. I kept thinking the longer we were there, the less likely it was that I would find them.

Don had to keep telling me they went to Fred's or that camp. Where else would they go?

I told him he didn't need to finish the search with me, but he made sure to tell me it was nonsense. "I have no plans. Why wouldn't I?" he said.

Holland and Jane became my friends in that time. Holland offered to come with us until it was time to meet the boat. He had decided he was going to Puerto Rico with Monroe.

It wasn't necessary that he come. I was sure Monroe needed his help and it probably would be easier for Don and me to go on our own. Besides, Monroe had told us he would get us within a two-hour drive of Fred's house. It wouldn't be long after our evacuation I would find my family. I took comfort in that.

The snowmobiles started going out just after the two-week mark. Not to look for survivors or pull some daring rescue, but to find an area where the helicopters could land. The roof of the hospital was useless. All roofs were. Many had buckled and collapsed from the weight of the ice.

The hospital was no different. The top floor was off limits and dangerous.

Finally, three weeks and two days after the storm, it was time to go. We would be evacuated in small groups of twenty on larger helicopters. Three choppers arrived at a time. It would take several trips and many days to relocate everyone who had taken refuge in the hospital.

Don and I were in the first round. Like everyone else we trudged in the cold carrying what little belongings we had.

The helicopter was bigger than the one I had ridden and crashed in before.

The young pilot wasn't wearing a coat. "It's below zero," I told him. "Why are you not wearing a coat?"

"It's warmer where we're going," he replied. "You'll see."

"Like normal Georgia warm?" I asked.

"More like…normal end of winter warm. The snow has melted a lot down there."

"I can't wait."

We boarded the chopper. I was excited and nervous—half a day away from finding my family.

I was ready to go and felt calm, not fearful about another accident. Helen crossed my mind, her reaction to being on the chopper. Then I did something she would have been proud of. I did it for her. Before taking off, I asked the pilot for a life jacket. Then a second for my hips…just in case.

TWENTY-SEVEN

BOB ABBOT

I felt the difference in temperature not long into our flight. At first, I thought it was my imagination, but when I asked, everyone felt the same way. No longer was there a chill to my bones. A chill I thought I would take forever to lose.

"Be prepared to feel hot and sweaty," Don told me as we approached our landing. "We're layered. I have a feeling we won't need to be."

Granted, that statement had me thinking that we'd land to bright, sunny, seventy-degree weather.

I had the bright and sunny part right.

It wasn't seventy degrees. But compared to where we had been, where baseline temperatures were in the negative, it might as well had been seventy.

The sun was the one thing I loved the most. Seeing it and feeling it on my face. At forty-two degrees, I took off my coat not long after we stepped off the chopper. Carrying my backpack and Helen's was a lot easier without those layers.

I felt free.

It was so hopeful, reiterating the optimism I was feeling about finding my family. We were no more than a three-hour drive from Bainbridge camp.

There was snow on the ground, about three inches. The roads were slushy and I had no doubt they would only be wet by the end of the day. It was hard to believe the world up north was real and existed, that it wasn't a nightmare

We walked to the hanger with the others from the first trip, where volunteers handed us boxes. There were cots set up.

I didn't know what to do. Stand in line, grab one of those boxes? We hadn't been in the same chopper as Monroe and Jane, so I felt a little like a fish out of water. It wasn't for long.

"Mac, Don," Monroe called out.

We had just been standing there near the line. I looked up to the call of my name and saw Monroe waving us over. He stood with Jane who held a box. We walked over to them.

"You feeling okay, Don?" Monroe asked.

"Yes, sir, I am. I have had plenty of rest these last couple of weeks."

"Wish I'd had more time to spend with you up there. I was busy." He smiled. "Anyhow, I know you two are anxious to get going. Especially you, Mac."

"Oh, I am. I can't wait to see my family."

"I know that feeling. For all of your help with my daughter, this is the least I can do." He handed me a set of keys. "You'll see a military Humvee with the number 4422 on the side. These are the keys. It's a manual transmission."

"I'm good with that," Don said.

I handed the keys to Don. "You drive then."

220

"They want it returned," Monroe said. "I figured you can return it in Tallahassee, they'll get you back to Bainbridge or…"

"You can join us," Jane said, handing me the box. "Please. We put a list of authorized stops on the route to Miami. It would be good for your family, Mac. Please bring them."

"I feel like we're cheating," I said. "I mean, the rest of those from the north won't have it so easy."

"Don't be a martyr," Jane told me. "Take the opportunity. There will be a need for you there, we'll find one."

"I'll think about it." I glanced down. "What's in the box? It's heavy."

"Water, food and a radio. Even though there is one in the car," Jane said.

"Do you have your relocation papers?" Monroe asked. "You may be asked for them at the highway checkpoints and at the camp."

I smiled gently. "I do. We had two copies. Thanks to Helen. She put our papers in a plastic bag and one in my backpack. The other one is Glen's. I was surprised they were still safe."

"Good old Helen," Monroe said.

"She wouldn't have gone to Puerto Rico," I said. "I'm sure of that."

"Yes, she would have," Don added. "We actually talked about it the night she passed."

I turned to Don with surprise. "You never told me that."

"I told you we talked about a lot and the memories would pop up," he said. "And we should go." He extended his hand to Monroe. "Thank you for everything."

"No, thank you," Monroe replied.

He hugged Jane and thanked her, then I embraced them both one at a time.

"I'm gonna miss you, Mac," Jane said. "We'll be great friends if you come to Puerto Rico. Thank you again for helping me."

They both thanked us again before we left. It felt odd, because they did far more for us.

Jane was Monroe's daughter and he was happy to have her alive and back when he thought she was lost in a dark, cold world. As a parent, he couldn't thank us enough.

I was certain I would feel the same way when I met Bob Abbot.

<><><><>

Intuition never came easy to me, or else I didn't really know how to tap into it. I was always the person who never saw something coming. When it came to Uncle Fred's, though, I had a feeling. I knew that wasn't going to pan out. One, Uncle Fred was never home. He left the hot, muggy weather of Georgia in the summer and either went north or on a cruise.

He lived meagerly to have money to travel.

I didn't say anything to Helen, because she said the last she spoke to him, he was home.

Uncle Fred was flighty. He probably had a trip booked months in advance before the freeze, and went anyhow before all travel was suspended.

Who knew?

I did know and had a feeling he wasn't going to be at his house.

However, in normal fashion for me, I didn't see it coming that three families would be living in his two-bedroom, one-story modular home.

There was a man named Derrick there, along with his wife and baby.

He seemed shocked and a little defensive when I knocked on the door, tried the knob and called out, "Uncle Fred! Uncle Fred are you there?"

He swung open the door.

"Is Fred here?" I asked, thinking maybe it was a cousin or something.

"There's no Fred here."

"This is his house," I said.

"It's ours now." He shut the door.

I knocked again. I didn't call out, I just kept knocking.

Again, he swung the door open. "I told you there is no Fred here. It's our place."

Just as he went to shut the door again, Don extended his hand, stopping it. "The lady just needs to speak to you. She's looking for her family. You can understand how that is. There's no need for hostility."

The man nodded and opened the door to allow us in. That was when I saw all the people in the house. Fred's normal clean and quiet house was mayhem. How could one clean with so many people in so little a space?

"Do you know where the owner went?" Don asked.

Derrick shook his head. "No. We are part of the relocation," he said. "We were in a temporary camp. We just moved in here two weeks ago. Something about vacant property. If it's empty for two weeks, it is seized for refugees. They shoved a lot of us in here. I'm actually waiting for another place. This is better than sleeping outside though."

I looked around, there had to be at least four children that I could see. "Are these yours?"

"No, two of them don't even have parents. They just dumped them on us."

"No," a woman's voice called out. She stepped from the kitchen, holding a baby on her hip. "I said we'd take them. They're part of an orphan registry. Your uncle lived here?"

"Yes."

"I can tell you most of his stuff was gone. Anything of value was already gone. A neighbor said he left. He was trying to find his sister."

I closed my eyes and exhaled. "Thank you."

"Maybe he went to the camp?" Don suggested.

"Maybe." I looked at the woman then Derrick. "Thank you and good luck."

"Same to you," Derrick said. "I hope you find your family."

"Me too."

We needed to get going. We'd eliminated Fred's house; my family had to be in Bainbridge.

<><><><>

I didn't know what to expect from Bainbridge camp. I knew it was under construction when we were first assigned. The short highway stretch was the one and only time we were stopped and asked for papers. They merely glanced at them and sent us on our way, stating to look out for the signs.

RCGA-223 was spread out in a large field. It wasn't tents or trailers, it was a series of square buildings placed together in a horizontal Jenga. The structures looked as prefabricated as Fred's house.

It wasn't mass hysteria or chaos, there was a dirt parking lot with orange cones and a sign that indicated registration.

That was our spot.

The exterior of the building was plain. Like the others, it had a single door.

"Registration," I said, as we stood outside.

"You okay?" Don asked.

"I am. Just nervous."

"Don't be. You'll be with your family soon."

"You'll stay with us, right?" I asked. "You aren't leaving are you?"

"You have your family," Don said.

"And yours?"

"Mac. You know without direction I will never find them. Maybe, who knows, I'll go with Monroe."

"Well, Jane is cute," I said. "Maybe you two…"

"Um…no." He smiled. "Let's do this." He reached for the door.

"Here we go." I stepped inside.

The building was warm and a woman sat behind a desk. There were two people in front of us in line. I kept leaning to the right to see what she did.

She had a tablet, like an iPad, on a stand. Eavesdropping, she asked for names, took identification, instructed them on where they would go, how to get there, and where to stop for a welcome box.

It seemed to take forever, I just wanted to shout out, *Excuse me, I am only trying to find someone.*

But I didn't.

Finally, we were next in line.

She was pleasant, I didn't expect that. Somehow I figured after dealing with people all day she'd be miserable.

"Welcome. Your name?" she asked with a smile.

"Mackenzie Garret," I said and handed her the papers.

"Oh, I was just going to ask for those. You have them. Good job."

"Actually…" I said. "My husband and I got separated and I think he is already here."

"Even better, no registration screen." She touched the tablet. "Last name Garret?"

"Yes."

"There we are."

I looked at Don and grinned.

"Oh my God," I gushed. "I am so happy. He has no idea."

"Then he'll be glad to see you. A little walk," she said. "Building seventeen, unit four. It's a big unit. Big family."

"Actually, one of us didn't make it."

"Oh." She drummed up a look of sympathy. "I'm so sorry. But the children and your husband, Tony, showed up right before the storm."

My heart sank. "No, his name's not Tony. It's Glen."

"Maybe they have it wrong. Tony Garret…children ages ten, six—"

"No," I cut her off. "Could you look for Glen Garrett?"

"Common name. More than likely multiples." Her hands moved on the screen.

She didn't have a poker face. "I'm…I'm sorry. There's no Glen Garett here."

"Maybe," Don said. "Maybe they are stopped somewhere because of the storm. It's possible."

I nodded and looked to the woman. "Can you check for my children? Cleo Garret, Aaron Garret."

She looked at the screen. "I'm looking at all the Garretts that are registered. They aren't here."

"What about an orphan list?" Don asked.

I quickly looked at him.

"Mac, it's possible," he said. "Ma'am, do you have one?"

"If they came in and were orphans, they would still be registered, but their name would be in green. We have nine Garretts here. They aren't here."

"You're sure?" I asked. "No Cleo or Aaron Garret."

She shook her head as she looked at the screen. "No."

"How about," Don said, "Bob Abbot."

She looked up.

<><><><>

Since I first heard his name, I'd developed a picture of Bob Abbot in my head. In my mind he was older, more than likely bald, a thicker build with a beer belly and a hard look about him.

He did have a sort of rough look about him, but Bob Abbot was nothing like I'd pictured. He was in his thirties and had a thin body with a ruggedly handsome face.

He was wearing an eighties band tee shirt and baseball cap when we found him in the food distribution and stocking room.

The woman at the desk, Melanie, knew exactly who he was.

Bob Abbot must have been some special human being because everyone knew him and remembered him.

"Bob Abbot?" I called out when Don and I stepped into the storage room and saw him. It had to be Bob, he was the only one there.

"That's me." He turned around and smiled. It was such a genuine smile.

"Hi Bob." I walked to him. "I am so glad you're here."

He was still smiling as he extended his hand. "What can I do for you?"

"My name is Mackenzie Garret."

I knew.

I knew that second something was wrong. His grip on my hand weakened and the smile fell from his face the moment he heard my name.

<><><><>

I wasn't prepared.

At first, I was so hopeful. Especially when he said, "My God, you're alive."

I realized Glen had told him I had passed.

Then he said, "Let's go back here and talk."

He led us back to a small office. As we were walking there I realized Don felt something was wrong. He placed a supportive hand on my shoulder.

"Sit, please," Bob said.

"Why?"

"Please." He pulled out a chair for me and I sat.

"I was told you were with my husband," I said.

"Glen," he stated. "Yes. I was."

"Was?" I felt Don reach over and grab my hand.

"He said you were dead," Bob said. "He told me that you were washed away with the bridge. You and his mother."

"We were."

"So she perished there?"

I shook my head. "No. She passed away during a storm."

"I see."

"Bob, you were with him?"

Bob nodded. "He broke my heart. I went back to help after the bridge washed away and he was there, screaming and yelling, just

228

destroyed, watching the mudslide. He didn't want to leave, but I got him to."

Don said, "We followed your trail. We took the same route."

"Oh, yeah, he told me about this camp. Showed me the papers," Bob said. "I told him to come with me. I thought I could get him some help."

I felt the ache in my chest. I didn't need to hear it, but I had to ask. "Where is he? What happened?"

"Glen...Glen loved you so much," Bob said. "We talked, you know. He talked about his family and how he adored them. How at least you and his mom didn't go alone. He loved you. But he couldn't live without you."

"What happened?" Don asked.

"Glen...Glen couldn't do it. We were at a camp, on the second day. A hundred miles, maybe less, from Baltimore."

I hurriedly looked at Don. "Sam. Sam's camp. He wanted to talk to me."

"Yes, Sam, he was at that camp," Bob said. "Glen...Glen took his own life. He...hung himself. I'm so sorry."

I felt the pain in my chest and it caused an aching groan. It made sense to me at that second, Sam's reaction to me. He had something to tell me, Glen's death was it.

I wasn't prepared. Not at all. I was hopeful that my husband had traveled with a man with a stellar survivor reputation. But even Bob Abbot's skills couldn't save him.

Glen had died.

I couldn't believe it.

"No!" I shook my head. "No. Glen loved me, yes, he loved his mother, but he would never take his life. He loved his children more than anything."

I felt an entire internal collapse of my soul when I saw the expression on Bob's face.

"Mac," he said so gently and reached for me. "He couldn't live without any of you. The kids…the children…are gone."

TWENTY-EIGHT

TOMORROW

My soul and my heart wanted to scream, *No!* loudly in agony and pain. Cry out from the depths of my being as I dropped to my knees in an uncontrollable release of grief. My heart felt the grief, but my head…it told me a different story.

It was one of the very few times in my life I wasn't blindsided; my head saw it coming and I simply replied with a, "Thank you. Thank you for telling me."

Bob Abbot was a wonderful human being and was deeply affected by Glen's passing. He had wanted nothing more than to help, but Glen saw no means of help. He had witnessed his wife and mother being washed away. Then, according to Bob, he watched as Cleo jumped from Aaron's arms and ran toward us when she saw the truck being swept from the bridge.

My son, always being protective of his sister, raced after her, lifted her and Glen watched as they, too, were swept away. My only consolation was that my children had felt the pain of loss and death only for a brief moment.

We stayed with Bob for a little bit, listening to him recount Glen's last days. How he was so broken.

I understood that. I knew the pain. I didn't have to witness what he did and I supposed it, the loss of his family, had stayed with him every time he closed his eyes. It would for me.

I even understood why he ended his life. I wish he would have held on and hoped for something, because had he done so, he would have found me. Instead, I found nothing.

They gave us a unit, not the one intended for us. There was no need. No longer were there five people. It was cute and plain, reminding me of mine and Glen's first apartment.

Even though there was furniture, I sat on the floor doing what had become my nightly routine since Helen had passed. Every night I'd hold that boot as I emptied the contents of Helen's backpack, looking at each and every item, breathing in a little of her.

"Here," Don said, extending down a green mug. "Drink some tea."

"Thank you." I accepted it, sipped it, then placed it next to me.

"Are you hungry?" he asked, sitting on the floor with me.

"No. You're not going to scold me and tell me I need to eat for my strength, are you?

"Not yet. Skipping a meal or two right now isn't going to kill you."

"I'm beginning to think nothing will," I said. "Lord knows I put myself in enough situations where I should have."

"None of us can assume to know why we are chosen to live and others are not."

I lifted the mug and took another drink. "I feel so much loss right now, Don. The pain just…just feels too big for my body. I can't imagine living like this."

"I can't imagine you will always feel this much pain. It won't go away but you'll learn how to live with it," he said.

"Will I?"

"People do. They have and they will. In this world especially, so many have lost so much."

"A part of me just wants to die."

"I understand that. You don't need me to tell you that it would be such an injustice to your family's memory if you did. Someone needs to keep them alive. That is done through memories."

"I'm not going to kill myself," I said. "I'm not. As much as I don't want to live, I am far too much of a coward."

Don chuckled softly. "A coward? You are the bravest woman I know. Every minute you survive this pain shows how strong you are."

My grip tightened on the boot. "I knew, you know. The second, the second we found this boot, I knew. I wanted to dig." I lifted my eyes to him. "You said we needed to go. Did you know? Did you feel it?" My focus went back to the boot.

Don shook his head. "No, Mac, I thought your family was alive. There was no doubt in my mind. Helen…Helen did not."

Hurriedly, I looked at him again. "When did she tell you this?"

"The day she died. She asked me if I thought she was a bad person because she didn't feel like they had survived. She said she felt she'd lost her son."

"Is this another memory you just recalled?"

"No, Mac, I never forgot she said that. I just didn't tell you and I'm sorry for that."

"Don't be. The thought of finding them kept me going."

"Then they weren't really gone, were they?" Don asked. "They guided you."

"But now they're not."

"Yes, they are. They led you here. Now you just need to find where they lead you next."

It was too soon to know where that would be. A part of me didn't want to be led anywhere. I was empty. Completely empty. I had lost everything. Glen, Helen, my children were truly all I had in the world. I'd had nothing before them and now I faced nothing without them.

I had to decide eventually if I could pick up the pieces and move on or allow myself to be as cold and dead inside as the world around me.

Sitting on the floor with what little physical memories I had, I just didn't know what to do. All I knew was I felt duped. Like I entered a race and finished first to find out no one cared.

No prize. No glorification for trying. My goals were met with heartache.

On that day when the rivers washed us from Glen and the kids, Helen and I had begun a search. One that kept us going, motivated and alive. A search for our family. She found them, I didn't.

At least one of us succeeded, one us had that reunion, one of us…was happy.

It wasn't me.

TWENTY-NINE

TODAY

Curaçao
Four Years Later

"Don's back," his little voice said.

But he had to be mistaken, it was far too early in the day. Vinnie had to be wrong, he probably hadn't even looked. I know I didn't. Knees to the ground, I was focused on my gardening and preparing for another harvest.

I raised my head and wiped the sweat from my brow. It was seventy-five degrees and it felt hot. As I glanced up, I saw Vincent run by.

"Stay away from the ledge," I warned him. "I mean it. You fall down again, I'm not getting you."

He laughed.

That's what five-year-olds did. Laugh. He didn't have a care in the world, and I was happy about that.

In the aftermath of the loss of my family, I just couldn't stay at that camp. As nice as it was, as nice as Bob Abbot was, I had to go. I had two choices: I could leave and search for something, or I could meet Monroe and Jane in Miami.

Don and I chose the latter.

The day that we showed up for the boat, I saw the looks on their faces. They expected to see my family. They helped me so much in those days of early grief. They grieved with me.

Life was different. Monroe as the vice president was leaving the country, not for a better life, but to try to get the southern hemisphere to help. To take on some of the refugees, put us to work in farming. Anything, because the United States was done for as far as agriculture. At least for a good year.

The boat was far from majestic; in just shy of a cargo ship we sailed for Puerto Rico. I felt like I'd cheated, that I didn't deserve such a beautiful place. Not when my fellow countrymen were starving, freezing and dying. I escaped the horrors while they still lived them.

Only the southernmost portion of the United States was livable and since the freeze had become overcrowded.

We received word constantly of unrest and anarchy.

It wasn't long after we arrived in Puerto Rico, four months, just after Christmas, that Venezuela offered to take in refugees. Ten thousand to start. Over time, more countries opened their borders.

I spent a lot of my time learning about agriculture, that's what I wanted to do. Grow things, see life again.

I couldn't shake the death. Not until a global effort went into effect to find homes for orphaned children— the Orphan Initiative.

There weren't enough families to take on one or two children each, let alone families that wanted to take them. Monroe told us they were looking for couples willing to create a family environment. Not for just a few children, they were talking group homes. Where children would be made to be part of a large family.

While Don and I weren't a couple that early, we were inseparable as friends and by the six-month point post-freeze, we needed another focus.

They said there would be perks to being an Initiative Family. The home, the land, the commodities, they were nothing compared to the perks of giving me back life.

Vincent wasn't the first child we took in, but he was the youngest. He was under a year old. He couldn't walk and he would never know the world that the other children remembered. He would never know any other parents other than me and Don.

One year after the freeze, we had been given eight children, a piece of land, and a home on the island of Curacao. The government provided us with most of our food and we worked on the bartering system for the rest.

Don was a teacher and taught at the school in our village. I stayed home and took care of the kids. I also focused on my gardening, which had become profitable in the bartering system over a couple of years.

"Don's back," Vincent announced again.

He couldn't be. It was his week off and all Don had wanted to do was go out fishing after he went to trade. I took off my gardening gloves, stood, brushed off my knees and walked to the staircase that went down to the pier.

Sure enough, Don was there taking something off his boat. He looked up to me, smiled and waved. After I returned the wave, I went back to my gardening.

The kids all ran about. Life was carefree for them. Like normal, they hated school even though Don was their teacher. The older ones were lazy and just liked to lay around when they weren't creating a mess.

I caught Don's shadow over my plants before he spoke. "Why didn't you wait?" he asked. "I waved."

"I waved back. I wanted to get this done for trade next week," I said. "Kids are a handful today."

"Really. They don't look like they're acting any different than usual."

"Exactly. A handful."

"Today was report day," Don said.

"Was it?" I looked at him.

"It's the tenth. I heard the report when I was at trade."

"And?" I asked.

"Nothing. No change."

He referenced the freeze and the northern land affected by it. Every month, scientists measured the ice to see if it was melting. Four years and the temperatures were still at arctic levels and the ice showed no signs of change.

"Not a bad thing," I said. "God knows what will happen if it suddenly decides to melt."

"I think we know what will happen," Don said.

"We do. Hopefully it will happen long after we're gone," I said. "I don't want to be living in a water world or telling our grandchildren, 'Dry land is not a myth, I've seen it.'"

Don laughed. "That joke doesn't get old. Here." He reached down.

I finally completely stopped what I was doing and looked. "Whoa." I took the bottle Don handed to me.

"Burt's finest. He said not too much at once. It's like two hundred proof if that's possible."

"How much?" I asked.

"Two pockets."

"Wow, good price. I take it trade was good?" I asked.

"Yeah, it was a great day, actually. Trade went fast, I was out on the water before I knew it. The fish were finding me. Strange. We'll have a pretty good feast tonight."

"How fast was trade?" I asked.

"Less than an hour. They wiped me out superfast. I got some good stuff. You have to come back to the house and see," Don said. "Your harvest is popular and in demand."

"Well, everyone loves my special plants."

"Pot, Mac, call it what it is. You grow pot."

"I grow good pot."

"Yeah, you do. Okay, I'm going to unload. See you back at the house soon?" Don asked.

"Ten minutes."

"Works for me." He reached down, first running his hand over my hair, then leaning down to place a gentle kiss on the top of my head.

I returned to my plants and laughed when I heard him holler out, "Vincent, didn't we tell you about staying away from that ledge. No, I'm not. Get up."

Laughter.

In the early days after my loss I never thought I'd see a time where I would laugh again. Laugh, smile, love...live.

But I did.

No matter how many years passed, not a day went by that I didn't think of Glen, Aaron, Cleo, and Helen. That I didn't miss them with all of my heart, yearn for them.

The children, Don, they didn't replace my family, they were additions to a family I just didn't see anymore. I didn't have a new life, I had a different life.

And life…life was different. Just like Glen and the kids, I would never see our home again, and more than likely, never see the United States again.

It just wasn't going to be possible. I heard things got better in the US, but where we were was removed and I wanted it that way.

It now was home.

Although I wasn't completely healed, I was working on it. I just had to keep my head up, keep going, keep living. It would keep getting better and life did go on.

The thing that helped me the most was what I learned. My story wasn't the snow, the displacement, the frozen land or devastation. My story was about the journey, where and who I was and where I was going.

I only needed to look around me for proof that the journey wasn't over, not yet…and not by a long shot.

ABOUT THE AUTHOR

Jacqueline Druga is a native of Pittsburgh, PA. Her works include genres of all types but she favors post-apocalypse and apocalypse writing.

For updates on new releases you can find the author on:
Facebook: @jacquelinedruga
Twitter: @gojake
www.jacquelinedruga.com

Printed in Great Britain
by Amazon